Bumped Off at the Bake Sale

Saltcliff Mysteries
Book 2

Nancy Stewart

Chapter One

The last of the summer heat blew out of Saltcliff on the Sea along with the first fall storm blowing in. I'd lain awake the previous night as the wind had buffeted the Eucalyptus and pine trees lining the village streets and left strewn leaves and needles in its wake, and rivulets of rainwater washed it all into piles along Nutmeg, the main street in town.

This morning, Taco Dog and I emerged for our daily walk into a garden dramatically changed from the one we'd strolled through the night before as we'd walked and then locked up the Saltcliff Inn for the night. Stalks of flowers lay across pathways, petals were scattered around, and greenery was stripped or broken, as if a giant had wandered through on his way to a late-night engagement.

Taco whined as he nosed around his favorite blooming bush, and then looked up at me.

"Are you sad that summer's over, or that your garden is suddenly a disaster?"

My service dog's soft eyes held mine for a moment, and then he went back to nosing around. The truth was that my sister's beautiful garden, which greeted the inn's visitors as they arrived, had been in decline since her death. Though I was doing my best to take over her inn-keeping duties and to be a reliable and loving guardian to her daughter Diantha, my skill set did not extend to gardening, and the storm had accelerated the decline I'd been aware of for a couple months now.

"Right," I said, mostly to myself, since Taco was now pulling at his lead, eager to head out into the village to see if any of his friends were out and about this morning. "I think it's time to hire a gardener."

I'd been running the inn for the better part of six months now, and felt like I was getting the hang of it—both in terms of the day to day and in my understanding of the inn's financial position. We could afford a gardener, and since neither Amal, the manager, or I had any gardening ability, it had officially become a necessity.

My English chocolate Labrador and I strolled the cobbled streets of Saltcliff, moving slowly past the storybook cottages with their curving rooflines and blooming window boxes. The air felt clean in my lungs, and despite the mess the storm had left, something inside me was eager for cooler days and nights, and all the things that fall would bring. The baking, for one thing, was always more rewarding in cooler seasons. I mentally ticked through my fall recipes as we walked, but when a brightly colored figure appeared ahead, my thoughts were interrupted by Taco's pull on the leash.

"Doll, you survived!" Sylvan called down the sidewalk on Nutmeg.

"We did," I answered, appreciating my friend's electric pink rain jacket, which he'd paired with royal blue galoshes and a pair of lime green pants. "How about you?"

Sylvan leaned in and kissed my cheek as his Basset Hound, Luigi, greeted Taco. Luigi was wearing a set of blue galoshes to match his owner's, and I suppressed a giggle at the ridiculous sight. Taco glanced up at me as if to thank me for not subjecting him to that particular humiliation.

"We lived," Sylvan said, removing his sequined sunglasses, which were shaped like stars. "The yard is a disaster. Branches and leaves everywhere."

"The wind was surprisingly strong," I agreed.

"Excessive, if you ask me," Sylvan said, looking annoyed that no one had consulted him about the strength of the wind before unleashing it upon us.

"What are you up to this week?" I asked, inwardly pleased that my small talk skills had improved enough that this conversation didn't feel awkward and stilted, as pretty much every chat I'd had in the last forty or so years had. Keeping an inn and raising a tween had done a lot for my comfort level with people in general.

"Same as you, I'm sure," Sylvan said, again looking somewhat inconvenienced by whatever was going to be taking his time this week.

"Same as me?" Was Sylvan going to hire a gardener? I doubted it.

"The Saltcliff School Festival?"

Oh, that. I had seen signs. And Diantha had said something about this a day or two ago. And I might have dodged a phone call from Dorothy Withers, a teacher at Diantha's school who seemed to be involved in pretty much everything. The last time she'd contacted me it was to discuss Diantha's preference for black clothing and ripped fishnet stockings, and I'd decided that she was someone I didn't need to jump through hoops to speak to in the future. "Is that coming up soon?" I asked.

"Three weeks, missy, and I already know that you have a massive role to play this year." Sylvan waved his glasses and pointed them at me.

"I do?"

"Baking, Doll. That paltry PTA cannot continue putting out their measly spread of anemic, flat cookies now that you're here. And the bake sale is the best part of the festival."

"The whole town gets involved in the school bake sale?" I was surprised the average villager would care much about a bake sale put on by a local school.

"Maybe not when it started, but the bake sale began morphing into a full-blown festival a few years back, and now the whole town takes part. It's like a street fair that happens all over town—people put out booths and we block Nutmeg to cars so everyone can stroll. And at the end of it all, most people end up at the schoolyard for the bake sale for snacks and refreshments and the cake walk. I heard they're getting a Ferris wheel and bringing in that Neil Diamond cover band to play this year." Sylvan looked more excited than I would have predicted about this last part.

"Oh," I said, not having realized the extent of the festivities. "I guess I'd imagined just a little school thing."

He shook his head. "People come into Saltcliff from all over the peninsula for the festival. It's the real deal, Doll."

My friend had taken to calling me "Doll" almost as soon as we'd met, and I did my best to push down the knee-jerk reaction I'd always had to anyone shortening my name. I knew it came from a good place when Sylvan did it.

"I guess maybe I should call Mrs. Withers back," I said, thinking aloud.

Sylvan made a face. "Unfortunately, she holds all the strings. She's been organizing the whole thing for a decade.

No one can pry it out of her talons, I'm afraid." He lifted a hand in front of his face and made it into a claw, making a horrible face as he clutched at air. "The old witch."

"What do you do at the festival?" I asked.

Sylvan looked surprised at the question, dropping his Mrs. Withers act to shake his head lightly. "We attend, Doll," he said lightly. "Luigi and I dress in our finest and grace the festival with our presence. Isn't that enough?" This was delivered cheekily, and I smiled at Sylvan's ability to be completely over the top and yet still warm and relatable.

"I'm sure it is," I told him, patting his arm.

"Well, this dog won't walk himself, unfortunately." Sylvan slid his sunglasses back on before leaning in to kiss my cheek again. "Ta!"

"Ta," I said back, feeling immediately silly. I was not a woman who said "ta."

"It sounds like we have some things to figure out," I told Taco, turning us back toward the inn. I needed to see if baking was the reason Mrs. Withers had phoned. That, I decided, could be fun. I'd been looking for a way to get a bit more involved at Diantha's school, anyway.

Taco and I stepped back through the front door of the inn to find several guests serving themselves the breakfast I'd laid out before my walk, with Amal looking on from the reception desk.

"Morning," she said, offering me a wide smile.

"Good morning." I hung up the leash and checked in with a few of our guests to see that everyone had what they needed, and then joined her at the desk. "How are you?" Amal remained a bit of a mystery to me. She had been part of the package when I'd taken over the inn after my sister's sudden death, and if not for her, I'd have had no idea what I was doing most of the time. She was also the steady hand of continuity my niece had needed through the difficult time after her mother had passed.

Amal was tall, elegant, and beautiful—all things I definitely was not with my mousy brown waves and glasses. She was also graceful and mysterious, a woman I still felt I barely knew, despite having been in Saltcliff with her for nearly six months now.

"How was the walk?" she asked now, scrolling through upcoming reservations at my side.

"Good, if you don't count the tree limbs and leaves everywhere. That was quite a storm," I said.

She glanced at me. "It was. Scary?" Her dark eyes were concerned.

It struck me as odd for a moment that she thought I might be afraid of storms, though I knew many people did harbor irrational fears related to all kinds of external things. My phobias, however, were largely limited to the confounding workings of other people.

"Not especially," I said. "There were plenty of big storms out east. I'm used to it."

"And Taco?"

"He doesn't mind much as long as there's dinner on time and someone to scratch behind his ears now and then."

Amal laughed at that and a warm glow lit inside me. Our relationship was comforting and easy. I might not have known Amal well, but I treasured her nonetheless. The fact that she had been close with my sister in the years when I was not added to my warmth for her.

I was about to ask something in return about how Amal's little cottage had fared in the bad weather, but the apartment door that separated my house from the main floor of the inn swung open, and my niece appeared.

"Morning," she said sleepily in the direction of the desk where Amal and I still stood. She didn't look at either of us, instead proceeding with her morning routine, which usually involved greeting Taco with lavish affection and sometimes rolling around with him until he was uncontrollably excited and needed another walk and Diantha was covered with fur.

"Try not to get Taco worked up, please," I said. "I need to chat with you before school."

Diantha looked at me now, her brown eyes widening as she turned to glance over her shoulder.

When I'd first met my niece, she'd worn excessive amounts of dark makeup, especially around her eyes. Amal had suggested that it might be her form of mourning her mother, and I'd done my best to disregard the makeup. It had very little to do with the person beneath it, after all. Over the past few months, Diantha had used less makeup, and had grown out the unnaturally dark color her hair had been dyed so that it was a very pretty chestnut brown, which glinted with highlights beneath the soft lobby lighting.

"Am I in trouble?" Diantha asked, rising to face me.

"What? No," I said quickly.

"I thought she was in trouble too, by the way you said that," Amal said, laughing.

"Oh. Sorry." I'd gotten better at the casual interactions required daily between us all, but inflection and nuance were still not my strong suits. And sarcasm was still a mystery entirely. My twin sister had been the relator between us, and even though I'd spent many years living in the world on my own, my skills hadn't improved much.

"No, no trouble," I assured them both. I followed Diantha to the side table, where she began loading a plate with blueberry muffins. "Eat some eggs and fruit too, please."

She glanced at me and rolled her eyes, an expression

that was clear enough to need no translation at all. Despite the heavy sigh, she took several strawberries and blueberries and a scoop of scrambled eggs.

As she sat, I poured myself another cup of coffee and sat next to her, greeting the couple at the far end of the dining table as I did so. It was the Khouris, a friendly, quiet couple from the desert down south. He was in the military, I thought, and she was some kind of marketing contractor. They came to Saltcliff regularly to escape the heat and wind, from what they'd told me.

"Mrs. Withers called me," I began, and Diantha suddenly dropped her head to the table next to her plate with another sigh. Twelve-year olds, it turned out, were very dramatic. "Not about you, per se," I continued, and Diantha lifted her head.

"That old grump hates everyone, Aunt Dolly. Whatever she said, you have to keep that in mind."

"Well, I didn't answer when she called," I admitted. "But I suspect it's about the bake sale."

Diantha's eyebrows lifted. "Oh, well, yeah. That makes sense. Ever since you sent those cookies to school with me for Mr. Bentley after his dog died, everyone talks about them."

Mr. Bentley was the principal at the Saltcliff School, and if there was any human emotion I did relate easily to, it was the love of a dog. I couldn't imagine losing Taco.

"Plus," my niece went on, pushing a piece of muffin

past her lips even as they were trying to form words, "oo atta epp ow aa best ner tow."

I waited, tilting my head to one side. "Swallow," I suggested.

Diantha did so, patting her mouth with a napkin. "Sorry. Those are really good." She pointed at the muffin. "I said you're kind of well known around town since all the guests talk about your baking when they go out."

Ah. That, I knew, was true. In fact, Valerie Killeen from Beachside Bakery had told me recently that she was glad I wasn't selling my baked goods because she feared I'd put her out of business.

Baking had always been a comfort to me, something I turned to when the world outside the kitchen didn't make a lot of sense. The mathematical simplicity of measuring and mixing didn't require interpretation and there was no risk of humiliation if I got something wrong. Very different from the world of people—for me, at least.

"Well, I just wanted to be sure it would be okay with you if I offered my help," I said. "I don't want to step on your toes."

Diantha's eyes held mine for a long minute, and then she smiled softly. "I'd like that. Thanks for checking with me."

I kissed her forehead gently, a rather new show of affection for me, but one she seemed to like. "I'll call her back today then."

I got up and began tidying up the breakfast area, and a few minutes later, Diantha was pulling on her backpack and heading out the door.

"Have a great day, Danny," I called as the door swung shut behind her.

Chapter Two

That morning Amal and I had several guest rooms to turn over, and then, in the break between check outs and check ins, she suggested we get a quick bite to eat out in town.

"That's a great idea," I agreed, latching on Taco's leash. So far, I hadn't encountered any legume-laden dishes, which was the whole reason Taco and I had gotten together in the first place, but having him by my side when I tried new foods was always a reassurance. Taco was an allergen dog, but he was also my best friend. I liked having an excuse to take him everywhere, if I was honest about it.

Together, we walked up Nutmeg, which sloped gently downhill as it traced the path through town to the Pacific Ocean. We walked up the hill, stopping by silent agreement outside Beachcomber Bites, a deli I hadn't tried yet.

"Your sister loved this place," Amal said, as we took our

number to a table out front and sat to wait for our sandwiches.

Every mention of Daisy struck a little tender spot inside me. My twin and I hadn't really spoken in ten years before she died, and the grief I felt mingled with regret whenever I thought of her. I considered the way I'd essentially stepped into her life after she'd passed. And now I found myself living in her house, raising her daughter, running her inn. If only I could have heard from her what had led her to that decision—to appoint me guardian.

"It looks incredible," I said, gazing around at the sandwiches, soups, and salads being enjoyed by other diners.

Taco sat obediently at my side, also gazing around with drool hanging quietly from his jowls. He was the most selfless Lab in the world, I thought—because he smelled my food for me, but never begged to eat it, as much as he would have loved every last crumb. His incessant drool was the only sign of his interior longing. I rubbed his ears, and swiped his jowls with his service dog bib, earning an adoring amber-eyed gaze.

"You have the same order," Amal said quietly.

"We do?"

"Daisy always ordered the French dip with a side salad. No chickpeas."

I thought about that. "When we were kids, chickpeas were one of the first things I reacted to, and Daisy swore them off in solidarity afterward." It was odd to think she'd continued to avoid them, even when she was avoiding me.

Amal nodded. "She talked about you often. Fondly."

"I want to believe you. It's just kind of hard."

"She was complicated."

I sighed. "We all are, though, aren't we?"

"It is not an excuse. I tried so many times to get her to reach out to you." Amal's voice trailed off, her eyes growing sad and misty.

I shook my head. "I didn't make an effort either, though."

"She never held that against you. She just...she worried. And then she'd let it go so long, she said, that it seemed impossible."

"Amal, how long did you know Daisy?"

"We met just after she bought the inn. She was planting the beginnings of that garden out front, and I was walking by. I stopped to say hello..." Amal met my eyes briefly, and then dropped hers again. "Dahlia," she began. "There's something—"

"I think I already know," I told her. I'd been thinking a lot about the things Amal had said about my sister, about the way she spoke of her. She loved her, I had no question in my mind about that. But suspected it was slightly more than that.

"You do?"

"Were you and Daisy... together?" I asked.

Amal hesitated, meeting my eyes again as if expecting some kind of judgment. Then she nodded. "We were in love. She was my person."

"And you were hers," I finished for her, my heart twisting in sympathetic understanding of what Amal had lost when Daisy died.

"I was hers," she agreed. She looked up at me again. "Does it bother you? Knowing that?"

"No," I answered without hesitation. "I'm glad she had someone to care for her. And that you did too."

Our sandwiches arrived then, and the motion created by the setting down of plates seemed to sweep away the sadness lingering over the table. I lowered my plate for Taco to investigate, and when he laid down beneath my chair with a groan, I set it back on the table and joined Amal in enjoying lunch.

We were just cleaning things up when Amal waved at someone approaching.

A small, round-cheeked woman paused next to our table, smiling at us both. "Hello ladies," she said. "Good to see you, Amal. Sorry to interrupt your lunch."

"Oh no, we were just finishing up. Betty, this is Dahlia Vale, Daisy's sister and Danny's guardian. Dahlia, Betty Bennett. She runs the PTA at the Saltcliff School."

"Hello!" Betty said, more loudly than I thought was necessary. "I've been meaning to come meet you, Dahlia.

Mr. Bentley has glowing things to say about you. And about your cookies."

"Er... Nice to meet you," I said, and reached my hand out awkwardly, realizing too late that this might not be a hand-shaking kind of hello.

Betty gazed at my hand, and then reached her own out and took it, shaking my fingers nervously before giggling. "Anyway," she said, as if to brush the strange handshake away. "I'm glad to run into you. Mrs. Withers suggested you might be just the person to head up the organization of this year's bake sale."

"Oh," I said, surprised. "I'd planned to contribute, but organize it?"

Betty waited, her wide-eyed expression never faltering.

"I, uh. I suppose, maybe..." I was looking for a way out of the responsibility, but Betty did not appear prepared to offer one.

"Sure," I said finally, and my acceptance seemed to reactivate Betty's ability to speak.

"Wonderful! I'll tell Dorothy right away, and we'll be in touch! Hope you're up to it, it's going to be our biggest yet. And Dorothy Withers is quite specific about how she likes things done. Thank you, Dahlia!" Betty turned partway through this excited speech and began walking away, giving me little chance to respond.

"She's a master, isn't she?" Amal asked when Betty was gone.

17

I shook my head, feeling like I'd just been run over by a PTA bus. "A master?"

"At getting people to accept jobs they have no intention of accepting."

"She is, I suppose," I agreed, wondering what had just happened. "She just... she just stood there and I talked myself into it."

Amal smiled, nodding slowly. "It's pretty impressive." At my concerned expression, she added. "Don't worry, Danny and I will help."

"Okay," I said slowly, worried I may have accidentally taken on too much.

After lunch, we strolled a little bit, with the intention of stopping by the Mutt Modiste to see how the sales of Danny's crocheted dog scarves were going. I'd promised to teach her to crochet the dog sweaters I'd been making for years, but we hadn't quite gotten to that level of expertise yet, and Danny had been so excited, she'd talked Tabitha, the owner, into selling scarves.

"Hello there, Taco Dog," Tabitha called from behind the counter to the side of the little shop as we walked in. I'd noticed that she greeted the dogs as if they were the customers, saying hello to the people only if she had time. "Hi," she waved to Amal and me.

"Hi Tabitha," I said, approaching. "We just wanted to see how the scarves are selling."

Tabitha made a face. "No one wants a dog scarf," she said. "But I couldn't tell Danny that."

I understood. I couldn't see a situation where I might put a scarf around Taco's neck either.

"That's too bad," I said. "It'll make her sad to hear it."

"Don't tell her that," Tabitha said quickly. "I'll buy them, and she doesn't need to know." With that, she pressed a button, opening the register on the counter, and began counting out bills.

"That doesn't seem right," I said, and Amal joined me at the counter.

"It doesn't," she agreed. "Tabitha? I think Danny will understand. It's a lesson—supply and demand, understanding the customer."

Tabitha paused in her counting and tilted her head. "She's just a kid. And she just lost her..." she trailed off, looking sadly between us.

"Maybe there is something else she can create that will sell better," I suggested. "Something that would be fairly simple?"

Tabitha put a blue-painted fingernail to her lips. "You know, a couple people have mistaken the scarves for leashes at first. They seemed excited about colorful woven leashes."

I turned and picked up one of Danny's scarves. "I think that's possible. If she could do them narrower, with strong colorful twine, maybe?"

"That might work," Tabitha agreed. "But we'd need a clip at one end, and a handle at the other."

I replaced the scarf. "I think we can manage that," I said. "But maybe it would work best if you suggested it to her? This is her venture, and I'd like her to feel in control of it."

"Oh," Tabitha said, looking unsure.

"Just tell her what you told us," Amal suggested. "That customers are really looking for leashes, and that you think these could be very successful with a few modifications."

"I'll help her figure out the details," I said.

"Okay," Tabitha agreed. "She won't be upset?"

Amal shook her head. "I don't think so. Not if you offer an opportunity along with the bad news."

"We can send her by later this week," I said, and Tabitha agreed.

As Amal and I strode back toward the inn, a cool breeze blew through town, bringing a distinctly autumnal scent with it. "You did well there," Amal said.

"I did?"

She nodded. "I"m not a parent, but I think your

instincts are good. That Danny will benefit from handling her own affairs this way."

"I hope so," I said. "I have no idea what I'm doing, if you want the truth."

"I suspect many biological parents feel that way too," Amal said.

I wondered if that was true. No one got a manual when they had a baby, I supposed. And we probably learned mostly from how we'd been parented ourselves.

Luckily, Grandmother was a stickler for treating children like small humans rather than coddling them like incapable babies. She'd always spoken to Daisy and I in a regular tone, often using words we had to stretch to comprehend. But to my young mind, that had felt like trust and confidence—she didn't limit us or our worlds. Instead, she'd guided us calmly into her world of adults and responsibility, so that we were ready when she left us.

It was what I was sure my sister had been doing for her own daughter, and something I'd try to take over gracefully.

As Amal, Taco, and I arrived back at the inn, we entered the garden gate to find a familiar figure lounging on the bench to one side.

"I'll see you inside," Amal said, giving my arm a squeeze as she headed under the curved archway into the inn.

Owen Sanderson stood as he spotted me with Taco, a

wide smile displaying the dimples on either side of his handsome face. His aviator shades blocked his emerald green eyes, but I'd seen them paired with that smile enough to know they were sparkling.

"Hey Dahlia," he said, the smile never faltering.

"Hello Owen." I stood a few feet from him, still not quite sure how to handle the warmth that flooded me every time I was the subject of his attention. "Is there some official police business I can help with?"

He laughed, and removed his shades, and I almost wished he hadn't. Owen in aviator shades was handsome. Owen with those bright green eyes fixed on me was incapacitating. "Yes, actually."

A little part of me deflated. Of course this was an official visit. Owen was the police detective in Saltcliff, and we'd worked together on a recent murder case—unofficially, of course. Still, some little bit inside me must have hoped this was a personal call. I had a gigantic crush on the detective, but I found it nearly impossible to understand how to navigate it.

Taco pulled the leash forward and stuffed his head against Owen's thigh. Taco did not suffer from social awkwardness.

"How can I help?" I managed.

"I was hoping you would agree to have dinner Saturday night. In an official dinner-having capacity, of course." As he spoke, he walked slowly down one of the garden paths, and I walked with him, Taco sniffing eagerly around us.

Owen's words caught me off guard. How would dinner qualify as police business? "I, uh... is this part of a case?"

"Nope. But policemen have to eat, so that's official police business. And I'd like to take you out."

"Like..." I stammered, unable to articulate my thoughts.

"Like a date," Owen confirmed. "I am asking you out on an official date." The green eyes gleamed hopefully, and Owen looked the tiniest bit uncertain, the big shoulders sagging just a fraction of an inch as he waited for me to answer.

"Oh," I said, surprise and shock making me unable to reply appropriately.

"Oh?" Owen's shoulders fell just a bit more.

"I. Um. Saturday?"

"Saturday. It's the day after tomorrow. Is that okay? Do you have plans?"

"No plans, no." Accept, Dahlia. What was wrong with me?

"So, is that a..."

"I would like to go on a date with you to dinner Saturday night," I blurted.

Smooth. Very smooth.

Owen's shoulders pulled back again, making him look every bit the strong, capable detective I hadn't been able to stop thinking about since we'd first met. "Great." He patted Taco's head. "Think Taco wants to come?"

I hesitated. Taco always went with me to restaurants just in case there were legumes in something I was served. But I hadn't taken him on a date since I'd gotten him. Mostly because I hadn't been on a date in the past four years. Dating was not part of my usual retinue of activities.

"He usually eats out with me."

"Well, then, he's invited too."

"Okay," I said. Would it be odd to bring one's dog on a date? I would ask Amal.

"I'll pick you up at six-thirty? We can walk. I thought we'd hit the Captain's Table."

The Captain's Table was the nicest restaurant in town, since the Cliffside had closed down a few months earlier after the chef's unfortunate death.

"Okay," I agreed. "See you then."

Owen winked at me, and then turned on his heel and strode confidently out of the garden. I watched him go, nerves and excitement battling one another for centerstage in my chest.

I let out the breath I'd been holding and headed inside. I opened my mouth to tell Amal about the date, but she and another woman sat on the couch in front of the fireplace, which glowed with a low fire, and both turned to look at me as I stepped in.

"Dahlia, this is Dorothy Withers. She's the English

teacher at Saltcliff School and heads up the Saltcliff Festival and Bake Sale each year." Amal stood, and appeared somewhat relieved to wave me into her spot on the couch.

"Hello," I said, realizing it was already quite late in the afternoon if school had ended. Diantha would be home soon. I sat in the spot Amal had vacated, pushing my excitement about Owen to one side so I could focus on the stern, stony-faced woman in front of me.

"Hello, Ms. Vale." Dorothy Withers stuck out a hand, which I shook, relieved to understand that this was, in fact, a hand-shaking occasion. "I understand you have agreed to head up this year's bake sale."

"I, uh..." How had Betty gotten the news to her so quickly? "Yes."

"Wonderful." Dorothy Withers produced a fat manilla folder from the bag at her side and spread it open on her lap. "Everything you will need to know is in here. We will require at least thirty varieties of baked goods, no more than four fruit pies, and at least fifteen cakes in order for the cake walk to be entertaining. Cookies must have at least two feature ingredients, with the exception of the sugar cookies I, myself, bring each year. Those are indicated here." She pointed a manicured finger to a spot on the list she'd pulled from the pile of papers.

"Tables will be spaced around the school soccer field at the optimum distance from one another, which we have determined over the years is three feet, and tablecloths must be cloth, not plastic, and contain no yellow or red, so as not to attract wasps. The school has three booth structures, which you may offer to those with the most appealing items."

The door to the inn opened as Dorothy Withers continued explaining the excruciating minutia of the bake sale, and Diantha appeared. She grinned when she saw me, but the smile dropped the second she spotted Mrs. Withers at my side.

"Diantha," Mrs. Withers said, looking up. "I meant to speak to you about that skirt today."

My niece wore a short purple denim skirt over tattered tights, paired with heavy-soled black boots. I'd grown accustomed to her style, and even kind of liked it now. Her shirt, at least, was colorful, and she'd stopped wearing the dark makeup around her eyes, choosing a pink gloss and a coat of mascara most days instead.

"It looks nice, doesn't it?" I suggested, not eager for Diantha to be scolded in her own home.

"Actually," Mrs. Withers began, but I cut her off as Diantha's little face fell.

"Danny, could you give Taco his dinner early, please? He got rushed through breakfast and he's desperate." My very non-desperate dog perked up at the mention of dinner, raising his big head from his paws as he lay at my feet.

"Sure," Diantha said, smiling as she looked down at Taco. "Come on, buddy." Taco leaped to his feet and joined her at the door that separated our apartment from the lobby of the inn. "Nice to see you Mrs. Withers." With that, Diantha and the dog disappeared through the door. I glanced at Amal, who was typing something at the registration desk, and noticed her subtle smile.

I was winning at this parenting thing today.

"Well," Mrs. Withers said, clearing her throat. "Let's go over the budget."

"Sure," I agreed, settling in.

"I want you to know that the accounting this year will be meticulous. I will accept nothing less."

"Of course," I said, feeling pinned under her beady-eyed gaze. Did she think I was going to steal from the school?

After another hour of Mrs. Withers talking incessantly and pointing to numbers on her many spreadsheets, she rose. "I'll see you at the school tomorrow at eleven-thirty for the walkthrough, then."

"I, uh. Yes. Okay. See you then."

And as Mrs. Withers left, I realized I really had become a part of this town. I was needed here in a way I'd never really been needed before. It was a nice feeling.

Chapter Three

The Saltcliff School was a small public charter school perched atop a cliff on the northern side of Saltcliff on the Sea. Though it was a school, the expansive, lush grounds were used for many town functions, which I supposed was why the bake sale for the school's PTA had morphed into a whole-town festival over the years. The soccer field where I would set up the sale opened via gates right onto Coriander Street, which led straight to the heart of the village.

I parked in the staff parking lot as directed, still not quite used to driving my sister's electric blue Fiat. I'd been managing, but the car was a stick shift, something I understood in a technical sense, but I found that practical operation was a tiny bit more nuanced. I did not bring Taco along this morning, and would almost certainly have felt somewhat naked without him, were I not juggling three tins of cookies, which Mrs. Withers had demanded she be allowed to sample before I could commit to making them for the bake sale.

The car door was easy enough to close with my hip, but I nearly tripped over the curb as I looked around at the buildings, trying to figure out where the English room might be. Mrs. Withers had taken for granted that I'd been to the school before, and for some reason, I hadn't wanted to correct her.

"Woah there!" A man's voice floated over the pile of cookie tins I was balancing, jovial and full of laughter. "Need a hand there, miss?"

I didn't have a chance to answer one way or another another before the man was taking two of the big tins from my arms.

"These are heavy, aren't they?" he continued, his rich voice carrying a hint of glee. "And do they smell heavenly? Oh my."

"Thank you," I said, finally able to see the red-haired older man who'd kept me from dropping cookies all over the ground. I couldn't help that I liked him rather automatically since he'd addressed me as "miss" instead of the elderly sounding "ma'am."

"They're cookies, for the bake sale."

The man had red bushy eyebrows to match his mop of red hair, and bright blue eyes set deep in a well-lined face.

He wore overalls and a name tag that read, "Angus" and below that: Janitor.

"Cookies, eh?" The grin widened. "Bake sale's not for another two weeks." His smile faltered. "Withers, I'd wager?"

We stood on one side of the parking lot, smiling at one another. "Yes," I told him. "And if you might be kind enough to point me to the English room to see her, I'd be happy to let you have some—I think I have too many. She wants to sample them to make sure they're up to snuff for the bake sale this year."

Angus's jovial smile dropped. "Course she does." The words were practically spat out. Then a smaller version of his smile returned. "Happy to point the way, but I'll not be going in with you if that's where you're headed," he said, lifting his chin.

"Oh, well, that's okay," I said, not sure what had changed his mood so suddenly. Not a fan of Mrs. Withers, I took it. I was beginning to sense that he was far from alone in that sentiment. "If you'll just steer me in the right direction..."

"Follow me," he said, a cautious note in his voice as he led me across a concrete open area between buildings, and then down a hallway covered by an awning. He pointed toward a door at the end of the hallway. "It'll be just in there," he said, and as he made to hand me the boxes back, the door he'd indicated swung open.

"Ah, there you are, Dahlia," she called, lifting her watch dramatically to eye level and squinting at it. "I'd worried you would be late."

I was never late.

"And you," her tone turned sharp. "I've been meaning to have a word with you, Angus. Come here."

"Aw, now we've done it," Angus whisper-moaned.

He took the boxes back from me and we proceeded together toward where Mrs. Withers stood, arms folded across her chest and her face set in a scowl.

"I'm not late, I don't think," I said. "I'm sure I gave myself plenty of time—"

"Angus!" Mrs. Withers barked as we neared the open doorway. "Come in here and see what a mess you left after your so-called cleaning last night." She waited until we'd both entered and then stormed in behind us.

Angus lowered his boxes to a desk and I did the same, feeling awkward as Mrs. Withers fixed her glowering stare on the janitor.

"The corners of the room were dusty again, and when I ran my fingers along the window sills, what do you suppose I found there?"

"Dust, I expect," Angus said, his tone low, defeated.

"Dust. That's right. Full of bacteria and parasites, no doubt. I also asked you to use that antibacterial wash on all the door handles and desks first thing so the smell would dissipate before I had to be in here again in the morning, breathing the fumes. But you didn't do that, did you?"

"Ma'am, I—"

"Never mind. I know very well you didn't. I've lodged yet another complaint with Principal Bentley, and you should be very, very careful at this point, I'd say. You're on quite thin ice, and if you think there aren't multitudes lining up to take your job, well, then, you'd be wrong. Very, very wrong."

Just as Mrs. Withers finished this warning in a screeching tone, the door opened again, and another man stepped in. "Is everything all right in here? I heard yelling."

Mrs. Withers spun, her face red. "I'll ask you to mind your own business, Mr. Thomas."

The man lifted his hands as if to show he meant no harm. "Just checking in."

"Well, in the future when you think you might like to check in, just refrain!" Mrs. Withers replied.

At this point I'd shrunk into the corner against the door, and wished I could actually disappear. I'd never seen one woman manage to make the atmosphere in a room so completely oppressive in such a short time.

"You got it," Mr. Thomas spit out before turning on his heel and heading for the door again. But he paused as he opened it. "And maybe you could lay off Angus. Screaming at him on the daily is not going to help anything."

"Good day, Mr. Thomas," Mrs. Withers snapped.

Angus had managed to inch back to the door during this exchange, and now he slipped through, giving me a half-hearted smile as he escaped with the other teacher, leaving me alone with a red-faced Mrs. Withers.

"Well," she said, uncrossing her arms. "I assume these are the samples of your baking?"

"Yes," I said, afraid to add anything unnecessary that might set her off. Diantha had complained about Mrs. Withers, but I was certain I hadn't understood the full extent of the woman's nastiness until now. She was clearly a miserable person. I wondered what in the world had happened in her life to make her this way.

Mrs. Withers popped all three tops off and peered into the boxes I'd brought. "Why on earth did you bring me so many?" She narrowed her eyes at me, shaking her head as I continued to press my back to the wall. "And why are you standing way over there? Show some pride in your baking. Tell me what I'm looking at."

I cleared my throat and pulled myself tall. I'd delivered briefs in front of officials at the Pentagon in my previous job. I could certainly handle one middle-school English teacher. Slowly, I approached the first box.

"These are my grandmother's icebox oatmeal choco-late chip cookies."

Mrs. Withers sniffed and daintily picked up one cookie from the box. I realized as she took the smallest bite I'd ever seen that bringing four dozen of each cookie was definitely overkill.

"Adequate." She dropped the remainder of the cookie into the garbage can at the side of her desk. Perhaps this explained how she maintained her sticklike figure.

"This one is a caramel apple sandie," I said, pointing to the second box.

Mrs. Withers repeated the performance with the second cookie, agreeing that it would do.

"And this is a triple chocolate cake cookie with butterscotch."

Mrs. Withers sniffed and stared at me. "I would have preferred something with pecans or walnuts for the third offering," she said.

"I don't eat nuts," I explained. "I'm allergic."

"Well, I don't expect you to eat them. Just to bake them, Dahlia."

I shook my head. "I'm very allergic to nuts and legumes. I never have them in the kitchen." When Mrs. Withers's expression didn't change, I went on. "I even have an allergen dog who usually goes everywhere with me. Taco Dog. He is an English Lab, and he—"

"There will certainly be no dogs at the bake sale!" She crossed her arms again and lifted her chin.

"Oh. Well, I'm sorry, then. I suppose we should have talked about that yesterday. Taco goes anywhere I might be exposed to allergens."

"There will definitely be nuts at the bake sale. Whether you use them or someone else does." Mrs. Withers had moved behind her desk and was gathering papers together. "I had hoped you were up to this task, but it's clear I'll need to find someone less sensitive to—"

"I can manage the bake sale," I heard myself say, more forcefully than I could remember speaking recently. "My dog is well trained and will not be a problem. I said I would do this, and I will." And, I didn't add, it would be the best organized and most successful bake sale the school had ever had. This had become personal.

Mrs. Withers stopped fussing over her desk and stood up straight again. "Very well," she said. "Your baking seems acceptable, at least. We'll see how your organizational skills are, and whether this mutt of yours will be a distraction. I fear I'm making a terrible mistake in allowing you to proceed, but alas... I have few other options." She sighed.

"Taco is pure bred," I said, feeling offended on his behalf over her derogatory use of the term "mutt." Of course, many of the dogs Taco considered friends were not pure bred, so I was insulted on their behalf as well.

"Fine."

"Fine." I put the lids back on my cookie boxes. "I'll just be going now," I told Mrs. Withers.

"Good night." The woman made no move to help me or to open the door for me, which resulted in a much less coordinated storming from the room in determined fashion than I would have liked. But I made it out the door, took a deep breath, and headed for the office.

"Oh, hello there." The secretary behind the tall desk seemed to be about to depart for the evening, her bag on her shoulder and keys in hand.

"Hi," I said, juggling my boxes. "Sorry to bother you so late. I just have all these cookies, and wondered if there is a staff lounge perhaps, where I might leave them for the teachers?"

"Oh, well, we never turn down cookies," the woman said, her face lighting up. "Here, let me help you." She took a box and then led me through a door to the lounge. "Samples for the bake sale?"

"Yes," I said, setting the boxes along the far counter where she indicated.

"Did they pass muster?" she asked, her eyes dancing. She evidently knew about Mrs. Withers and her requirement to test everything herself.

"They were deemed adequate," I told the woman.

"High praise. Mrs. Tuttle ran out of here this morning in tears because her apple turnovers were too big, too flaky, and too messy."

"Aren't those the things you look for in an apple turnover?" I asked.

The woman shrugged, and peeked into a box. "May I?"

"Of course," I said. "Help yourself."

"I'm Rosamund," the woman said. "Are you Danny's guardian?"

"Her aunt, yes."

"Oh, this is heavenly." Rosamund sampled one of the chocolate cake cookies and smiled. "She mentioned you'd be running the bake sale. That's a big job, especially taking into account who your boss will be."

"Mrs. Withers is..." I searched for an appropriate descriptor. "Tough."

"She's a raging you-know-what." Rosamund picked a cookie out of the second box. "She's made enemies of half the staff, and she's actively trying to get most of them fired. I guess she thinks she could run the school herself."

"She doesn't seem to like the janitor either," I ventured.

"Oh, they hate each other."

It seemed like Mrs. Withers hadn't heard the old adage about flies and honey.

"And after she called the school board on Principal Bentley, he's not a big fan either. She's even got the parents irate, though there are those who support her for an admin position."

Rosamund's desire to chat seemed to be fueled by cookies. She was on her fourth as she told me about Mrs. Withers's recent aspirations to edge out Principal Bentley. She also mentioned that the woman had received death threats from more than one parent based on grades they perceived as unfair.

"Wow," I said, unable to imagine threatening a teacher just because she gave Diantha a bad grade.

"Wow is right," Rosamund said around her fifth cookie. Then she took my elbow and steered me out of the lounge. "We need to get out of here or I'll eat every last one of those cookies. Thank you for those, and for agreeing to run the bake sale."

"You're welcome," I answered, and thanked her as I headed back out to my car. It seemed I had my work cut out for me.

Chapter Four

"It sounds like you've bitten off a pretty big job there," Owen laughed as I finished explaining the details I'd gleaned so far about my responsibilities at the school.

"I don't think it'd be a big deal at all, if Mrs. Withers wasn't determined to make it one."

Across the corner table in the restaurant, Owen's eyes were even greener than they were in the sunlight. The candle flickered low between us, soft music played, and the murmurs of other diners created a soothing background that made it feel a bit like we were alone. My initial nervousness had settled as we'd been seated and each ordered a glass of wine.

Now, partway through a second glass and all the way through my spaghetti Bolognese, I was very much at ease.

"Dorothy Withers," Owen said, drawing the name out and leaning back in his chair as he lifted his Brunello to his lips. He took a sip and swallowed, setting the glass back on the table before continuing. "She must call the station at least once a week."

"Really? About what?"

"You name it, but mostly about her neighbors. She doesn't like her neighbors' pets, is unhappy with their failure to deadhead their rosebushes, and thinks a quiet period should be made law from six in the evening until noon the following day."

"Well, you really should deadhead roses," I offered, having learned at least this much in my efforts to manage my sister's garden in front of the inn. I was unsurprised by the rest.

"Perhaps," Owen allowed. "But she is one of those people who seems unable to be happy. It'd be hard to live like that, I think."

I nodded. That would be hard. "I understand, in some ways."

"How?" Owen asked, tilting his head so that a lock of blond hair fell across his forehead. "I can't imagine you bitter and angry like that."

"But maybe I would have been," I say, offering him more about my past than I had before. "If I'd stayed where I was. I didn't have friends, really, and didn't engage in the world. I worked, ate, walked Taco, and slept. I wasn't unhappy necessarily... but I wasn't happy."

Owen's eyes held mine, shining and dark. "I'm so glad you came here, then."

"Me too," I said, and I felt the smile on my face deep in my chest. "I just wish Daisy were still here..."

"I know, I'm so sorry."

I'd told Owen before about the estrangement between my twin sister and me, about what a surprise it had been to receive notice that I'd inherited guardianship of not just my niece, but the inn as well. It would be Diantha's, but not until she was twenty two.

When the waiter came to ask about dessert, we were so deep in conversation, I'd almost forgotten where we were.

"I don't think I could eat another thing," I confessed.

"Just the check," Owen said.

"I'll pay my half," I told him, pulling my purse from its place at my side.

"Dahlia, that's not how this works." Owen said. "It's a date. And I asked you. So it will be my honor to buy you dinner."

"Oh, erm..." Hearing Owen remind me again that this was a date somehow made it seem more real, more meaningful, and suddenly I couldn't find the right words and I wasn't sure where to put my hands. I twisted my napkin in my lap.

Owen signed the check and then fixed me with a smile.

"Thank you," I said.

"My pleasure."

We rose, and I regained some composure as we stepped from the restaurant onto the sidewalk while a bracing breeze swept up Ginger Street from the Pacific below.

"Would you like to walk a bit?" Owen asked.

"I would," I said, and we turned toward the ocean, Owen's strong presence at my side equal parts comforting and jitter-inducing.

Together, we strolled the quiet evening streets of Saltcliff. Most of the boutiques and bakeries were closed this time of night, even on Saturday, but the few bars and patios outside the restaurants and cafes spilled light and music into the cooling fall evening.

Leaves drifted around the sidewalks from the trees shedding their coats for winter, while the evergreens interspersed still managed to make the village feel shielded from the elements. Like a secret enclave tucked away here on the coast.

As we turned to walk along the path that traced the cliffs above the beach below, Owen took my hand. His fingers were strong and masculine, something I'd noted before as we'd spent time together, and they were surprisingly soft, twined through my own.

A year earlier, if you'd told me that I'd spend a September evening walking along the Pacific shore, holding hands with a handsome detective, I would never have believed you. But this, I thought with a contented sigh, was my new life.

Eventually, we turned back, and Owen walked me through the garden in front of the inn, turning to face me at the door.

"Thank you for letting me take you out tonight, Dahlia. I enjoyed myself."

"Thank you," I said, looking up into his handsome face.

Owen still held my hand, and now he gave it a gentle tug, as if asking if I might like to step closer. I did, but as soon as he angled his head and leaned in, my nerves got the best of me.

The soft cocoon of our walk through the village shattered in the reality of his proximity and the abrupt worries that assaulted me about what Owen might expect exactly, what I might actually want, and whether we'd both end up ultimately disappointed, as tended to be the outcome of my interpersonal relationships. My sister included.

I turned toward the door, a sudden movement that had the effect of smashing my shoulder into Owen's chest as he leaned in, and pushing him back suddenly.

"Oof," he said, catching himself.

"Sorry," I mumbled, wishing I had more of my sister's charm and maybe slightly less skill with irrelevant things like theorems and algorithms. "I didn't mean to, I mean..."

My hand was on the doorknob, and I turned back to look into Owen's glimmering eyes. "Sorry. I'm bad at this."

The full lips I should have let kiss me pulled into another generous smile. "Dahlia," he said softly. "I'm in no hurry at all. I just like spending time with you."

The intensity of his gaze was almost too much, and my entire body felt hot. "Okay," I said. "Thank you for dinner. I had a really nice time."

"Good night," Owen said, and then he leaned in quickly and kissed my cheek.

"Good night." I hoped my furious blush was not obvious in the moonlight.

I turned the handle and stepped inside, relieved to find the inn's lobby empty of guests. But when I opened the door to the apartment, I had no such luck.

Three sets of eyes turned my way from the small den where Amal, Diantha, and Taco were watching television.

"Well?" Diantha asked, springing to her feet.

Taco Dog's tail thumped the carpeted floor loudly, but he seemed too content to get up, since Amal was sitting at his side, stroking him.

"How was dinner, Dahlia?" she asked.

"It was good," I said, putting my purse on the low table inside the door.

"Did you kiss him?" Diantha asked, grinning and wiggling her eyebrows.

Was this something I should talk to a twelve-year old about? "Um... no. But he kissed my cheek."

"That's sweet," Amal said, smiling.

I moved into the living room and took the armchair next to Amal. Taco lumbered to his feet now and dropped his head on my lap in greeting.

"Hello friend," I said, cradling his soft face in my hands.

"Do you think you'll go out again?" Diantha asked.

I met her eyes then. "I hope so," I said.

"That's wonderful," Amal said, rising to her feet. "I'm so happy you've found him."

I looked between them. "It was just dinner. Maybe we shouldn't get too far ahead of ourselves."

"Of course," Amal agreed.

But Diantha rolled her eyes and flopped back down on the couch with a sighing, "Whatever."

Chapter Five

I spent the next two weeks meeting with other bake sale participants, sampling their cookies, cakes, pies, bars, and reinvented turnovers, and reviewing logistics with Dorothy. Surprisingly, she'd relented and allowed me to take over her sampling duties, and even asked that I call her by her first name. I sensed that in Dorothy's world, that made us something like best friends.

"I don't know how you put up with her," said Valerie Killeen as we finalized the list of donations and the table map for Saturday's event. Valerie had become a baking buddy and friend, and had agreed to help me coordinate a bit, with the understanding that she would not have to interact directly with Dorothy.

"She's difficult," I agreed. "But I get the sense maybe she's just never been given the opportunity to be any other way."

"What?" Valerie said, her hands pausing in her counting of names on the very extensive donation list as we sat together inside the front door of her cafe. She laughed as she looked up at me.

"I just mean that maybe it's hard for her to know how to behave with other people, and somehow she settled into a kind of defensive demeanor. Maybe she felt like it kept her safe somehow?"

Valerie's eyes held mine for a long moment, and then she smiled softly and said, "I get the sense you're speaking from experience?"

I lifted a shoulder. "A little bit. We're not the same, but maybe I understand why she might have become that way."

Her gaze softened a bit, and her voice lowered as Valerie said, "Dahlia, I don't know you well. And admittedly, I don't know Dorothy well either. But I wouldn't put the two of you in the same category. Not in baking, not in friendship, and not in the kind of human beings I think you are."

Well. I felt the blush climb my face.

"Thanks," I managed to mutter. Friendships like Valerie's were new to me, and compliments like the one she'd just offered were unfamiliar. I had been told I was detail-oriented, hard-driving, focused, and tough. I'd never had a compliment about anything except my work. It was like being given a soft, silky little pillow to tuck into my pocket, something to pull out and rub my fingers against as a reminder that I wasn't quite the person I'd always believed myself to be.

I was about to say something else, attempt to return the compliment in some way, but was saved from the uncomfortable effort when Diantha pulled open the door, coming in from the street.

"How did it go?" Valerie asked. My niece and I had arrived at her shop together, but Diantha had come with the purpose of talking to Tabitha at the Mutt Modiste.

Diantha slumped into a chair next to Valerie, and Taco rose and dropped his head into her lap. She cuddled his soft ears and petted his head and then said, "Okay, I guess."

"What did she say?" I asked.

"Haven't made a single sale," Diantha moaned. "No one wants dog scarves."

"Oh," Valerie said. "I'm sorry."

"So, what does Tabitha want you to do?" I asked.

Diantha slumped lower. "She says people keep thinking they're actually leashes and that I should just make those." My niece's expression suggested that this idea was not a welcome one.

"Well," I said slowly. "That would be fairly easy to do, right? We could just—"

"I told her I don't want to," Diantha said, surprising

me. She avoided eye contact with me and rose again. "I'm going home."

Valerie met my eyes, and I suspected what I saw there was sympathy. For me? For Diantha? What I didn't see was a suggestion for the best way to handle the situation.

"Oh. Okay," I said, glancing outside as if I could ensure the streets would be safe for my niece to walk alone. This was Saltcliff. They were safe. "Sure."

Diantha had already stood, stomped to the door, and let herself out.

"Oof," Valerie said.

"I can't tell if she's upset," I said. "She seemed upset, but then she didn't say she was."

"I think it's safe to say she's not supremely happy," Valerie said. "But if you give her a little time, she might come to a decision about what she needs to do on her own."

I thought about that, picking at a crumb on the lemon muffin that sat on the plate before me atop the lists we were making. "Right." I realized it didn't really impact me either way if Diantha's project came to a quick halt, but I wanted her to decide for herself how to proceed. The thing I didn't know was whether that was the right choice. Is that what Daisy would have decided? Or would she go to the Mutt Modiste and try to smooth things over?

"Is it possible you're overthinking?" Valerie said, her soft voice interrupting my analysis of the situation.

I looked up at her, suddenly aware I might have

been sitting completely still, thinking, for a minute or maybe for an hour. "Yes," I acknowledged. "It's very possible."

She laughed lightly. "Well, let's finish overthinking the bake sale details, and then we can overthink what to do about Danny's scarves."

"Fair enough," I said, and when I leaned forward, pushing my plate aside, Taco groaned and laid down beneath my chair, clearly understanding that we weren't leaving yet.

We spent another hour ensuring everything would be set for the bake sale and festival this weekend, and then I scooped the layout and lists into my bag carefully and turned to say goodbye to Valerie.

"I'll see you at the school tomorrow afternoon for setup?" I asked. We were going to arrange all the tables and put up the tents so everything would be ready to go Saturday morning.

"I'll be there," she said. "And I promise not to say a snarky word to Dorothy, either."

"That'd be nice," I said, laughing.

"I'm glad she was willing to hand over the reins."

I wasn't sure I was, but I was pretty sure I wouldn't have been able to work as equal partners with Dorothy Withers if she had insisted on holding them. "Hopefully it'll go well," I said.

"It's gonna be great!"

The town was bustling as I strode home with Taco at my side through the quaint streets of Saltcliff on the Sea. People moved here and there over the cobblestoned roads, paused on the sidewalks to greet one another, and moved in and out of the shops and restaurants. The window displays were taking on a distinctly autumnal feel, with a few little sparkle lights popping up here and there, well in advance of the upcoming holiday season. Halloween was clearly the priority first, with pumpkins and broomsticks dominating much of the decor.

I, for one, was in no hurry to rush into the holiday season. I din't want to move through any day faster than it was meant to be lived. Now that my life was suddenly full of friends and people who needed me, I was enjoying my time more than I had in the last decade. My regained verve had come with the loss of my only family, though, and the holidays worried me. How would Diantha handle the first Christmas without her mother? How would Amal? Could I possibly hope to fill any part of the enormous hole my sister had left in their lives?

The inn appeared as I rounded the corner, deep in thought, and as usual I was calmed by the sturdy yellow brick of its front, by the sweeping arch of the garden gate that stood outside the extensive English garden my sister had planted.

"I still need to find a gardener," I told Taco, who looked up at me as if in agreement.

I let Taco linger a few moments near his favorite plants, and then we went inside, where he headed directly for his food and water dishes near the apartment door. He cast a doleful look my way when his food dish was found to be empty.

"You ate earlier," I reminded him.

He groaned at me and then noisily slurped at his water.

"How are the preparations going?" Amal asked as I rounded the registration desk to join her.

"Good, I think. Everything okay here?"

"For the most part. The Tennysons have asked to switch rooms."

I frowned. "Why? They don't like the Atticus suite?"

Amal sighed. "Mr. Brown. He's been active lately, I guess."

I did not believe in Mr. Brown, our resident ghost. Supposedly, he haunted the Holden suite, so it was the last one we ever booked and it was most often unoccupied. The Atticus suite was right next door.

"I moved them to Gatsby, but that means that when the Nguyens check in tomorrow, they'll be in either Atticus or Holden."

"Put them in Holden," I suggested. "Maybe with company, Mr. Brown will be quieter."

Amal frowned at me. "That hasn't usually been the case."

I'd heard the stories she and Diantha liked to share about Mr. Brown moving guests' belongings, playing with the taps, and turning on and off the lights, but I'd never witnessed anything myself. "At least if they have any issues, we can move them next door. If we start them in Atticus and they're unhappy, we have nowhere else to put them."

She nodded. "That does make sense."

"Amal," I said, lowering my voice so the guests helping themselves to tea at the side of the lobby didn't overhear. "Do you think it's odd to run an inn and have a room that you essentially cannot use to house guests?"

"I mean..." Amal nodded and shrugged.

"Is there something we can do about Mr. Brown?" It was hard to imagine procuring a service to rid ourselves of something I thought was imaginary, but I suspected that others would need the reassurance that the imaginary thing had been handled.

"Tessa Damlin might be able to help," she said, sounding uncertain.

Tessa was our next door neighbor, and the woman was a bit eccentric. She dabbled in things like fortune telling and seances, and while I didn't think any of it was real, it was still entertaining. She'd also helped solve the murder that had taken place here a few months back.

"I'll ask her," I said, making a mental note. "After the bake sale."

Amal nodded. "Good idea."

Chapter Six

The morning of the bake sale and festival, Diantha, Amal, Valerie, and I were all at the school's soccer field promptly at eight o'clock. Diantha was spreading table coverings—cloth, not plastic, and in shades that would not attract wasps—dutifully over each of the long tables, and Amal and I were greeting other volunteers who'd agreed to man the tables and help with processing payments.

It was quiet, for the most part, with just a few parents setting up their tables, since the festival would not begin until ten. Diantha and Amal had gone with a vendor to help blow up balloons, and Valerie and I were slowly getting our table ready to go. One of the booths had been offered to Mr. and Mrs. Franklin, and they were assembling it now, since Mr. Franklin had brought a whole case of tools with him and volunteered to build all three booths.

Unfortunately, Dorothy Withers was also here early, scanning the progress with a scowl.

I smoothed the tablecloth over our table and ensured Taco was seated beneath it, mostly out of sight, as she approached.

"I assume all is well, Dahlia?" she inquired.

"No reason to be worried," I said. "I'm certainly not expecting any issues."

"Well," she said, practically spitting the word. "The issues that matter are always the ones we do not expect." Her gaze floated over my shoulder to where Mr. Franklin was hammering something loudly.

"Must you make so much noise?" she called over to him.

The hammering stopped, and Mr. Franklin approached, handing the hammer to his wife as he stepped nearer. He was a big man with dark skin and close-cropped hair. He had a jovial nature about him when I'd met him before, but as he came near, his face lost all cheer.

"I've been meaning to speak with you, Mrs. Withers," he said.

"John, maybe not now," his wife called, looking worried.

"Sam is a good boy," he went on, ignoring his wife. "He works hard, pays attention, turns in his work on time."

"That is debatable," Mrs. Withers sniffed, not backing down even a centimeter.

"You gave him a failing grade on his last three assignments," Mr. Franklin went on. "He thinks you intend to fail him. You know he has As in all his other classes?"

"Perhaps he exerts more effort in his other classes," Mrs. Withers said, sounding bored.

Mr. Franklin's dark skin reddened and his hands clenched at his sides. "I've had several polite conversations with you, Mrs. Withers, but I'm wondering if there is some other way to phrase my concerns that will actually get through to you."

"Your son is not paying attention in class. That is not my fault," she said.

"He is a good boy!" Mr. Franklin roared this. "You've decided you don't like him, and you're punishing him. Why?"

Mrs. Franklin stepped close and took her husband's arm. "John," she said softly, trying to pull him away.

"No!" He jerked his arm free and pointed a finger in Dorothy's face. "You will treat my son fairly. You will disregard whatever preconceptions you have of him and you will grade his assignments based on merit, not on your own twisted prejudices and petty irritations."

"Sir, I resent your implication," Dorothy said, throwing her chin up. "I am a fair and experienced teacher, who—"

"You are a bitter and angry old woman who should retire before someone retires you!" Mr. Franklin shouted in her face.

"John!" Mrs. Franklin finally succeeded at pulling her husband away, and I watched as she spoke into his ear and then sent him back to the parking lot, assumedly to calm down.

"Well," Mrs. Withers said, smoothing her long skirt as if Mr. Franklin had ruffled her clothing. "That's gratitude for you. I don't see either of them agreeing to teach the unwashed masses." She sniffed and turned, heading off to check something else.

"Yikes," Valerie said, appearing at my side.

"Where did you go?" I asked. Valerie had disappeared as soon as Dorothy had strolled toward us.

"I was hiding behind the table," she said. "I didn't want a run-in."

"I guess you got one anyway," I said. "At least she wasn't yelling at me this time."

I sighed, and we moved back to the table, draping streamers in arcs across the front and arranging the platters and plates I'd brought to display our baked goods, but just as we prepared for the festival to open, Mrs. Withers appeared again, and Valerie began digging around in boxes beneath the table.

She needn't have bothered, however, since Angus—the friendly janitor I'd met the day I had first taken my samples to the school—waylaid her just a few feet from our table.

"Mrs. Withers," he said, adopting a more contrite

posture than he'd displayed the day I'd seen him in her classroom.

"What is it, Angus? We're very busy here today, as you can see. The festival is about to begin."

"Yes, that's just it," he said, wringing his hands in front of him. "There is a problem I think you'll want to see for yourself. I would hate for it to ruin the festival or anything."

She crossed her arms. "Problem?"

"I can show you," he said, pointing to the parking lot that separated the school grounds from the rugged cliffs that held the Pacific Ocean at bay.

Mrs. Withers let out a dramatic sigh. "I really don't have time for this," she complained. "But I also don't have time for future problems. Let's see what it is that you cannot handle on your own."

Angus didn't reply to her jab, but turned and walked with her in the direction of the parking lot.

"Whew!" Valerie said, popping up again. "That was a close one."

"Valerie," I said. "What do you think is going to happen if she sees you?"

Valerie gave me a sheepish smile and shook her head slowly, her voluminous red hair shifting around her shoulders. "I don't even know," she said. "It's a reflex. I've been hiding from Dorothy Withers since she failed me in ninth grade English."

"She actually failed you?"

Valerie lifted a shoulder and gave me a half smile. "I will admit that I was more interested in Donny Matthews two rows over than I was in Shakespeare."

I couldn't especially relate to that idea. Boys had never been a particular interest of mine, though Daisy had dated widely—but never had a serious boyfriend. Or girlfriend, I thought to myself, editing my understanding of my twin based on what Amal had shared. I definitely hadn't chosen boys over getting good grades, that was certain.

"It all worked out in the end," Valerie said lightly. "I can read and write a recipe and manage my books for the bakery. That's all I need!"

I watched my friend move around the table, adjusting the three-tiered display we'd set up for the cupcakes. She was pretty and fun, easygoing and optimistic. I had never had a friend like Valerie before, and as I considered her— and my luck and gratitude around my new life in Saltcliff —I felt a little glow of warmth inside me.

"Look, Aunt Dolly!" Diantha was running across the open area in the center of the field toward me, a bouquet of brightly colored balloons clutched in one hand and Amal walking behind her, smiling fondly.

"Wow, that's a lot of balloons!"

Diantha's wide smile stoked the glow I'd been feeling, and when she wrapped an arm around my waist and hugged me, the balloons squeaking and bumping one another all around us as they seemed to hug us too, I felt as if I might cry.

"Where should we put them?" Diantha asked, oblivious to the emotions I was struggling through. Amal had followed Diantha at a slower pace, and was standing beside us now. Her shrewd gaze caught mine and I knew she saw everything Diantha did not. She gave me an understanding smile and a nod.

"Let's split them into twos or threes and tie them on the table legs around the field," Amal suggested.

"Good idea," Diantha said, looking up at the enormous bouquet. "I might have gotten them a little tangled when I was running."

I swallowed hard and felt slightly more stable. "That's okay," I said. "We'll figure it out."

The next half hour was spent working with my close friends and my niece to finish setting up the festival. Soon we were ready to open, balloons bobbing merrily all around us and the California sunshine beginning to warm the brisk fall day.

Chapter Seven

The festival was busy. For hours on end, Valerie, Amal, and I stood at our table, selling treats and chatting with people who had come from Saltcliff and beyond to attend the festival. Diantha came and went, visiting with classmates and sampling other baked goods.

I tried to put eyes on some of the kids she seemed to associate with, wanting to know more about her life—my niece didn't confide in me about what went on at school, but some days she came home seeming unhappy.

At one point, a boy wandered by the table to say hello. He had longish hair that fell into his eyes and a shy demeanor.

"Hey Danny," he said, his voice lower than I'd expected it to be based on his lanky limbs and bright clear skin.

"Hi Caleb." Diantha's voice was neutral. I slid a glance at her, but she seemed neither happy nor annoyed to see Caleb at our table.

"These look really good," Caleb said, pointing at the chocolate cookies.

"They're three dollars each," Diantha said. "Or two for five."

Caleb dug in a pocket in his baggy jeans and came up with a five dollar bill. "Here," he said, offering it to me.

"Thank you," I said, handing him a plate. "Any two you'd like."

Caleb chose his treats and then said goodbye to Diantha with a shy smile. When he was out of earshot, she sighed dramatically.

"What's the sigh about?" Valerie asked.

"Nothing," my niece said. "Caleb's just so... weird."

I stared her. Weird was a term I'd heard a lot in my own childhood. Though I could embrace that weird was what I wanted to be a lot of the time now, it was hurtful when I was young. "Being different isn't a bad thing, Danny."

Diantha's eyes met mine and for a second I saw that she understood what I meant, but then defiance brightened her gaze. "Whatever. He's always lurking. He's even admitted to hiding around school before."

"Hiding?" Valerie asked.

"Like eavesdropping and stuff, waiting around corners,

ducking inside doorways." Diantha rolled her eyes. "Weird."

"Well, he seemed nice," Valerie said. "And you don't have to marry the guy. Kindness doesn't cost us anything."

"Marry him? Ew." With that, Diantha stood and let out another dramatic sigh. "I'm going to go check out the dunk tank."

Valerie and I exchanged a look of understanding as she walked away.

Besides the bake sale and cake walk, which both happened on the soccer field, there were a Ferris wheel and a carousel on the school playground, and the notes of a band warming up could be heard echoing on the breeze from the outdoor amphitheater at the other end of Coriander Street. The main gates were wide open, and the street that led into town was blocked off to traffic. Along each side of the street, local vendors had set up booths selling everything from handmade soap to honey, jewelry to cheese. There was even a hayride that left from the parking lot at the school and toured the town before completing the circle and unloading next to the booth offering free hot cider. The laughter and the excited shrieks of children punctuated the day.

Many of those who visited our table held pumpkins in their arms or pulled them in wagons, having dropped by the pumpkin patch set up in the quad.

"This is the best festival ever," Diantha told me later,

sitting in one of the folding chairs behind our table and sipping from a cup of hot cider. She alternated between helping at the table and exploring the festival on her own. She'd spent an hour with her friend Peyton, who'd stopped by to invite her to ride the Ferris wheel with her family, and then they'd checked out the vendors in town.

"I'm glad you are enjoying yourself," I said, still battling a surplus of emotion I wasn't sure how to handle. That had been one thing about my life before coming to Saltcliff—it was predictable. There were very few people in that life, and while it was quiet and a little bit lonely, I always knew what to expect.

"Has Mrs. Withers come over to check on Taco's behavior?" Diantha asked, sinking one hand into the thick fur below Taco's chin and scratching him. His eyes dropped shut and he let out a low rumble of pleasure.

I shook my head and gazed around. "No. I haven't seen her in hours, actually." I hoped whatever issue had arisen with Angus hadn't been a big deal.

There was a short lull in foot traffic around lunchtime, and Amal shooed Valerie and I away to find some lunch. "You two have been standing here for hours," she said. "Take a break and have some fun."

Valerie wiggled her eyebrows at me as she looped her arm through mine. "Let's go find some trouble," she suggested.

I did not want trouble, but I suspected she didn't really mean her words in a literal way. "Yes," I agreed. "But let's not get arrested or anything."

Valerie's eyes widened and her mouth dropped into a little O. "Good plan. We'll save that sort of trouble for non-school events."

We walked along the wide street, sampling treats and examining the multitude of goods for sale. There were many familiar faces in the crowd, but Valerie squeezed my arm tightly when we saw Owen approaching.

"Maybe we *should* try to get arrested," she whispered, giggling. "I wouldn't mind so much if he was the one to subdue me."

Her remark sent a furious blush into my cheeks just in time for Owen to see it as he came to stand in front of us. "Hello ladies. Are you having a good time?"

Valerie slipped to one side, showing sudden interest in the bolo ties on display in a nearby booth, leaving me alone with Owen in the crowd. "I am," I told him. "Are you?"

"I am now," he said, smiling. "Can I buy you a funnel cake? Or a corn dog? Have you eaten?"

"We just had corn dogs," I told him. "And in a minute I'll need to get back to the table."

"Do you have time to ride the Ferris wheel with me?" he asked.

I looked at my watch. "I think I do. Let me just tell

Valerie." I moved to where my friend was chatting with the bolo tie booth vendor to tell her.

Valerie wiggled her eyebrows when I said we were going to ride the Ferris wheel. "You know what happens on Ferris wheels, right?"

I did not. If the ride went as expected, very little happened, from what I understood. "No."

"He's going to kiss you, Dahlia!"

The tumbling feeling in my stomach that erupted whenever Owen was near increased. Did Owen intend to kiss me on the Ferris wheel? Did I want him to?

"Go!" Valerie said. "I'm going to head back in just a minute. I'll see you at the table." Valerie turned and nearly ran headlong into Principal Bentley, who was standing on the sidewalk looking a bit lost.

"Oh, sorry," he said, stepping to one side.

"Hello Principal," I said.

When Principal Bentley turned to me, he looked a little bit confused, as if he'd never seen me before, but then he quickly recovered. "Well, hello there. How are you doing?" He smiled pleasantly between Owen, Valerie, and me.

"Good, sir," I said. "Have you gotten to try many of the baked goods? I brought the cookies you liked so much after your—" I stopped myself, realizing that reminding a man about the loss of a beloved pet was probably not the right thing to do.

"Oh, I should go sample those right away," he said.

"I'm heading back up," Valerie told him. "I'll walk with you."

"Good, good," he said, glancing around before turning to walk at Valerie's side.

I turned back to Owen, who took my hand as naturally as if we'd been walking through crowds holding hands for years. It was comforting and thrilling and also so very confusing. Holding hands wasn't a big deal, but for some reason I felt like everything was moving very, very fast between us. I did not think I was ready to be kissed on a Ferris wheel.

Once we were in the little car, rising up over the crowd, I turned to Owen to express my concern. But I needn't have bothered.

"Do you see that?" he asked pointing down to the cove just coming into view at the edge of the parking lot at the school.

"It's pretty," I agreed. The tide was in, filling up the hidden coves with beaches that were only accessible via steep footpaths during low tide.

"No," he said, moving to my side of the car, and bending over more than I was strictly comfortable with. We were very high up. "On the rocks there."

I peered out where he was pointing. I did see something, a dark shadow piled on the rocks in the first cove, just above the water crashing onto the shore. "What is that?"

Owen frowned and took off his sunglasses, squinting down as the Ferris wheel turned, putting our car at the highest point. "That," he said grimly, "is a body."

Shock iced the blood that had been surging heated through my veins, and I forgot all about my plan to let Owen know I wasn't ready for Ferris wheel kissing. When he said the word, I could see he was right. The dark object on the rock had clear limbs now and I thought I could make out a head topped with dark gray hair.

Owen was immediately on his phone, and by the time we'd descended the Ferris wheel and had the ride halted so we could make our way across the school grounds and to the parking lot, there were already police cars arriving.

"Wait here on the field," Owen said to me, nodding at one of the men who'd emerged from a squad car. "I'm not sure if we can get rescue equipment down there with the tide in, we'll have to see." Together, they headed to the path at the far side of the parking lot that led down to the cove.

Diantha and Amal appeared at my side as I stood at the edge of the parking lot, Taco Dog with them. "What's going on?" Amal asked. I met her gaze to see worry mirrored in her eyes.

"I'm not sure," I said. "I think someone is down there. Injured, possibly." I recalled the figure I'd seen from the top of the Ferris wheel. The body had not been moving at all. "Or maybe worse."

Diantha stared up at me, her mouth dropping open. "Dead?"

I slid an arm around her shoulders. "I don't know."

Chapter Eight

The festival went on, most attendees unaware of the police activity going on at one side of the school parking lot. Most of the coves along the cliff line were well known among locals, but not visited often, thanks to the schedule of the tides. The first time I'd mentioned wanting to descend to see one, Amal had warned me that the coves were only exposed during low tide, and that the water came in fast as tides shifted. Only those who kept tabs on the daily tide schedule went regularly.

I didn't love the idea of racing the furious Pacific to save my life and my dog's, so I'd scrapped the idea of climbing down the steep paths for fun.

As I watched the police move around the entrance to one of the paths, I wondered about the person who had ended up down there. Had they fallen? Or mistimed the tides and drown, only to be washed up on the rocks? The paths were notoriously steep and could be muddy if the marine layer was thick, or if they'd been hit with sea spray.

"What do we know?" Amal said, coming to join me and speaking in a low voice.

"Not much," I said. "I think someone must have fallen on the rocks down there. I hope they're okay."

"I have Diantha helping Valerie clean up," she said. "So she's distracted for the moment."

"That's good," I said, just as Owen appeared over the top of the cliff's edge wearing a grim expression.

"He doesn't look happy," Amal said.

"No," I agreed. Owen's pants were wet from the knees down. He moved to converse with a small group of uniformed officers and then walked to where an ambulance had pulled up and was unloading a gurney. At whatever Owen said to them, they stopped what they were doing and pushed the gurney back into the ambulance. One of the men turned, following Owen back to the entrance to the path, while another returned to the truck's cab, where we could see him picking up the radio.

"I don't think they can get a gurney down there when the tide's in. They might have to get a helicopter or something. There's not a lot for us to do here," Amal said. "And if we don't want Danny watching the whole thing, we should probably head back to the inn."

I turned, surprised to see that the bake sale remains

had been mostly cleared, and the tables were being folded and stacked onto a flatbed truck that had pulled into the center of the soccer field. I realized I'd been standing here watching the scene unfold for the better part of an hour. Diantha and Taco were making their way toward us.

"What's happening?" Diantha asked me.

"I'm not sure," I said. "But we should probably head home and get out of the way."

"I want to know what's going on. Do you think the person is okay?"

"Danny," Amal said in a calm soothing voice. "I'm sure we'll find out soon. Standing here won't do any good for anyone, and we've had a long day as it is."

Diantha looked up at Amal and seemed poised to argue, so I added. "Plus, Taco needs dinner."

Taco tilted his head at me as I said this, his ears perking up. Dinner was one of the words he knew well, and he never seemed to tire at being used an excuse if it meant he got to eat.

My niece's shoulders slumped a bit, but she looked down at the dog at her side. "Okay, buddy. Let's go get dinner."

I checked in with the cashiers and glanced around to make sure no one needed my help. I did not want Dorothy Withers to hear that I'd left my responsibilities early, and was a little bit surprised she wasn't around to check in on everything.

Soon, we were loaded into the little car and heading back to the inn.

It was several hours later when my phone rang.

Diantha appeared at my side from nowhere. "Is it Detective Sanderson?"

I wasn't sure if her keen interest in whatever had happened at the cliffs today was healthy, but I couldn't blame her, either. I answered the call, hoping Owen hadn't been out there working all this time.

"Hi," I said.

"Dahlia," Owen said. His voice sounded ragged. "Sorry to ditch you like that. You got home okay?"

"We live just a few blocks from the school. We were fine. Are you okay?"

"I am, but I'm afraid Dorothy Withers isn't."

I sat up straighter, muting the television. We'd been watching "Stranger Things," but neither Diantha or I was paying any attention now. "What do you mean? Was that her, on the rocks?"

"I'm afraid so," he said, his voice weary.

"Why would she have been down there? Did she fall?"

"That's one possible explanation," Owen said. "I don't

know why she would have been climbing down the cliff in a skirt in the middle of her event, though. Especially just before high tide."

"I don't know either," I said, thinking back to the last time I'd seen her that afternoon. "Angus did ask to speak to her. He said there was some problem that might impact the festival. They walked in that direction, but I can't imagine that whatever he had to show her was at the cove."

"Angus? The janitor, right?"

"Yes."

"Well, I guess that's as good a place as any to start figuring out what happened."

"Owen," I said, turning my head away from my niece. "Do you think this was..."

"Maybe," he said, anticipating my question about foul play. "The coroner's report will let us know if the injuries are consistent with a fall or...something else."

"Will you let me know?"

"As much as I can, yeah. I'll call you tomorrow."

"Thanks." I hung up and turned to see my niece's worried face looking back at me.

"What did he say?" Her hands were dug deep into Taco's soft fur and I had a moment of inner joy as I realized how much my dog did for us all without even knowing it. He was an allergen dog, and he was good at his job, but he was also our friend and offered more emotional support to my niece than I was capable of doing myself.

"He's going to let me know the details tomorrow," I said, wondering how much I could keep from her.

"Is someone hurt?" she asked, her eyes huge suddenly.

I sat down at her side, reaching out to pet Taco as I considered how much to tell her.

"Someone is hurt," I said. "Actually, someone has died."

Diantha, much better at reading other people's unspoken words than I'd ever been, continued to look up at me through those wide brown eyes. "Someone we know?"

I nodded, sighing. "Mrs. Withers."

Diantha looked down then, her hands still petting my dog. When she turned to me again, the soft eyes were filled with tears. "I didn't want her to die," she whispered. "I didn't like her, but..." Diantha's face crumpled, and suddenly she looked so very young.

My niece began to cry, and part of me shrilled with shock when she removed her hands from Taco and reached for me, wrapping her thin arms around my waist and pressing her head against my chest. It took me a second to wrap my arms around her. I couldn't remember the last time I'd held someone while they cried. Had I ever? Maybe Daisy... my sister had been far more emotional than I ever was.

Still, it felt unfamiliar and comfortable at once, and as Diantha cried against me, I heard myself whispering to her. "Shhh, shhh. It's all right."

Taco pressed himself against my knees as I sat on the loveseat staring down at the little girl in my arms. My sister's daughter. My niece. A fierce and startling emotion rose within me, totally unexpected, but it was fiery and forbidding—I realized I would protect this child with everything I had. She was my family. She was... mine.

"I'm sorry, honey," I said after my arms had begun to tingle from holding one position for so long. "I know it's a shock."

Diantha pulled herself from me and looked up with a miserable, tear-streaked face. "I feel like it's my fault."

"What? How in the world could it be your fault?"

"I said I hated her."

"Danny. Words cannot kill people. And you never said that anywhere she could hear you, so your words could not have even hurt her feelings. Nothing about this is your fault. It sounds like it was a terrible accident. That's all." I hoped that was really true, but nothing about Mrs. Withers's death was sitting right with me.

Why would she have decided to hike down to the cove in the middle of the festival? In a long skirt? I doubted very much that her death was an accident.

Eventually, Diantha calmed down and I suggested we all get ready for bed. It had been a long day for everyone, even Taco, who flopped happily onto the rug in the middle of the living room, looking utterly spent.

Luckily, I had some frozen loaves of blueberry bread

I'd made that would thaw well for Sunday breakfast. I'd need to rise early to make a quiche and some bacon, but I was glad I'd thought to bake ahead a little bit. No matter what odd events went on in the town of Saltcliff, Sunday breakfast at the inn was non-negotiable.

Chapter Nine

Sunday morning dawned bright and clear, an oddity in Saltcliff in October.

"This bread is delicious," Mrs. Scolati said, coming back to the buffet for a second piece of blueberry bread. I guessed freezing it hadn't hurt it.

"Thank you," I said, doing my best to focus on the guests filling the dining room at the inn and not on waiting for Owen to stop by or call and fill me in on whatever he might have found out about Mrs. Withers's death.

The inn was currently full, partially thanks to the festival the day before, which drew visitors from all across the country, and partially because it was our busy season, leading into the holidays. Guests meandered around the lobby, refilling plates from the buffet and lounging near the fire, which we kept burning low almost constantly. Taco was curled into a circle on his bed near the apartment door, and Diantha picked at her quiche at the end of the big dining table. I was worried about her. She'd awoken still distraught about Mrs. Withers, and if I was honest with myself, I wasn't feeling great about everything that had happened at the bake sale either. Dorothy wasn't a happy person, but I didn't think she deserved to be killed.

I told myself it was certainly an accident, that she must have had a reason to go down the steep trail and she'd simply slipped. But even I wasn't convinced. Why would she have decided to hike down the trail in the middle of the event she'd worked so hard to put on?

"I'm telling you, Muffy is distraught," Mrs. Scolati was telling her husband. She held a very small dog in her lap--they were staying in the Holden, which was one of our pet-friendly rooms. Amal had worried that with the addition of Taco Dog to the staff in the lobby we might need to change our pet policy, but Taco had made it abundantly clear that he was not going to bother any of the guest dogs. He liked to say hello, but after the first encounter when Taco and a St. Bernard knocked over a side table and lamp in their greeting, we made it clear to Taco that shenanigans weren't allowed in the lobby. We also made a point of making sure he was in the apartment when dog guests arrived to check in whenever possible.

"That dog lives in the literal lap of luxury," Mr. Scolati replied. "What could she possibly have to be upset about?

"It's just a feeling I have," his wife said, frowning down

at the small white dog who didn't seem especially distraught to me. "Dahlia, dear, would you come here a moment?" Mrs. Scolati beckoned me over to where they sat. I put down the receipts I was entering into the system and crossed the lobby to see how I could help.

"Do you think Muffy looks anxious?" Mrs. Scolati asked me.

I glanced between her and Mr. Scolati, who appeared perturbed that this conversation continued despite his best efforts to end it.

"I think she looks..." I considered the little white dog, who had a black button nose and dark eyes, which blinked up at me. "She looks..." I did not have an emotive descriptor on hand for this dog, and felt the blush begin to climb my cheeks.

"Sad," Mrs. Scolati said for me. "See, Jeff? I told you. Dahlia agrees."

I looked between them, realizing my actual input wasn't needed here, at least not on Muffy's state of mind. "You know," I said. "There is a pet psychic up on Ginger Street. If you really want to get in touch with Muffy's feelings, you could try her. I've heard she's very good." Of course, I'd heard that from Tessa Damlin who was the only person I knew that was into psychically related things in any way. She'd done a very interesting tarot reading for me a few months back, and had actually helped solve a murder through a fake seance that she swore to this day had been real.

"Oooh," Mrs. Scolati said, nodding. "Good idea."

"That's ridiculous," Mr. Scolati said. "You think that's ridiculous, right Dahlia?" He looked up at me for consensus.

Oh dear.

"No it is not." Mrs. Scolati had adopted a baby voice and was directing it at her dog. "It is not at all, is it, Muffy? You want to tell us what's bothering you, don't you?"

Mr. Scolati blew out a frustrated breath. "Can't imagine what this is gonna cost," he muttered.

I excused myself and turned back to the desk, just as the bells over the door jingled, signaling Owen's arrival. My stomach did its weird little scramble at the sight of him, the sun chasing him through the open doorway and illuminating his golden locks. He was broad and strong, and he smiled every time he saw me--I thought he was the first person for whom that was true.

"Dahlia," he said, the smile widening. He stepped close and gave me a kiss on the cheek, which only served to worsen my blush.

"Good morning," I told him.

"Do you have a few minutes?" he asked, looking around the busy lobby. "I wanted to get your take on a couple things. Off the record, of course."

"Of course," I said. Owen had begun confiding in me as he'd investigated the murder in town this summer, but he'd made it clear that my assistance was purely unofficial, which was fine with me. I liked puzzles, but I certainly wasn't a cop and I didn't want to be. For now, I was an innkeeper and parent. And a failing gardener. I really needed to get someone over to take care of that.

I led Owen to a quiet corner where I could still keep an eye on everyone in case I was needed, and sat in the chair across from him. "Is it about the..." I caught myself before I said the word body. "About Mrs. Withers?"

He nodded gravely. "You saw her yesterday morning, right?"

"Yes. She checked in on everything at the bake sale before we got started."

"Did she say anything to you about going down to the cove for any reason?"

I shook my head. I still couldn't figure that out. Dorothy Withers hadn't really seemed like the outdoorsy type in the first place, I doubted she'd decided to take a moment to commune with nature in the middle of her biggest event of the year.

"That's the thing that doesn't make a lot of sense," Owen said. "Why she went down there at all."

"So you think she climbed down the trail for whatever reason, and slipped and fell?"

Owen shook his head, "Maybe. But my gut is saying that's not it."

"I'm sure your gut gets things right a lot, but is there any other way to be sure?"

"Funny." He grinned at me. "The coroner is cataloging the injuries. She'll be able to make a determination for sure."

"And have you spoken to the janitor, Angus?"

"We did talk to him. He said he'd talked to Mrs. Withers in the parking lot and then said goodbye to her there after letting her know there might be mice in her supply closet."

Mice. Ew. My brain began cataloging all the reasons why mice indoors were never a good thing. "Did he notice anything odd that he mentioned? Did she tell him she was going to go for a walk or something? What if Mrs. Withers was really afraid of mice, and she needed to go clear her head after receiving that news?"

Owen shrugged. "She just wasn't dressed for that climb. It doesn't make any sense."

"Want to ask Tessa to see if she can talk to her spirit and find out what happened?" I was half joking.

"Let's keep that in mind as a last resort. I just wanted to check in with you and see if you could think of any reasons Mrs. Withers might have gone to the cove, or see if you'd heard anything we could use. Mr. Bentley, the principal, suggested that maybe in her advanced age she was beginning to be a little... aimless."

"Aimless? Mrs. Withers was sharp as a tack. I wonder why Mr. Bentley thought that. I wish I could remember more about the morning."

I shook my head, feeling fairly useless. I'd been right there, and still, I didn't have a single tip we might use.

"That's okay," Owen said, and then his attention seemed to expand outward and his eyes caught on the buffet. "Oh, Sunday brunch."

"You're welcome to stay."

"Have you eaten?" he asked as his stomach rumbled loudly.

"I have, but I'll sit with you if you want to get a plate."

Owen grinned and rose to make himself a plate, filling it full of quiche and bread and then returning to where I sat, worrying about Mrs. Withers.

"Did she have any family?" I asked when Owen had sat back down.

He shook his head. "An ex-husband, I think. I'll track him down tomorrow."

Poor Mrs. Withers. I found myself feeling sorry for her as I sat there, trying to understand what her last motives might have been.

That evening, Amal stayed after the inn was officially closed to eat dinner with us and play Scrabble, something the three of us had begun doing regularly on Sunday nights.

Cooking had never been my strong suit, so we'd fallen into the habit of letting Amal make dinner while I supplied the dessert.

"I really don't know if I can eat another cookie after the bake sale," Diantha said when I offered her the plate of leftover cookies.

"I don't blame you." Even I was feeling a little bit sugared out.

Amal lifted a cookie from the plate with elegant fingers. "I always have room," she laughed.

As we sat around the small kitchen table, Taco at my feet and what little family I had gathered around me, I felt a sense of contentment. Life had changed drastically in a short time, but it all seemed right. If only Daisy were here too.

Amal seemed to be having similar thoughts. "Daisy would have loved this," she said softly, her eyes misty as she looked between my niece and me.

I wanted to believe her, but it was difficult. My sister

had quit speaking to me a decade ago, and I still didn't really know why. "I want to think you're right," I said, aware that my niece was listening with interest. "I hadn't talked to her in so long..."

A strange look passed across Amal's face and she dropped my gaze, toying with the letter tiles she'd lined up in front of her. Then she swallowed hard and lifted her chin again. "Daisy loved you," she said, her voice firm now. "She had reasons for the things she did. But never doubt that she loved you. Both of you." A tear stood in Amal's dark eye and a ripple of surprise ran through me at her fierce tone.

Diantha looked between us, her lips pressed hard together as her eyebrows lowered and her chin wobbled. "I miss her," she said softly.

Taco was already at her side, gazing up into her face as if volunteering to take away her sadness.

"I know, honey," Amal said, reaching a hand to take Diantha's.

"I still don't understand how she... it was so fast." Diantha sniffed, shaking her head.

I didn't know much about the circumstances around my sister's death. It had been cancer, Amal said, and it had been swift. I'd left the details alone, mostly to preserve Diantha and Amal's feelings. They both knew my sister much better than I did at the end, and it didn't feel right to turn up all those painful memories.

At least she'd left me this. A new life with people I loved. It was so much more than I'd had before.

That night as I got ready for bed, I allowed the sadness at my sister's absence to wash through me. I pulled on my loose pajama pants slowly, wishing somehow things had been different, that I'd at least had some explanation for the sudden way Daisy had cut me from her daily life. But she was gone, and there was nothing left that could explain things.

"Time for bed, Taco," I said, petting Taco's big soft head once more as he stopped his roaming of the room to let me say goodnight to him. Taco didn't sleep in the room with me. He had a bed in my bedroom, but he never managed to settle into it. I told myself he preferred being close to Diantha out of a feeling of responsibility for both of us. Tonight, though, he seemed even more uncomfortable in the bedroom than usual.

I shook my head. "It's okay, buddy. You can go."

Taco was nosing around the corner of the room, something he did often when he was with me here, and I stepped over to see what he was pawing at. "There's nothing there," I told him for the hundredth time.

But he stared up at me and whined, and then he glared at the corner and barked three times.

I shook my head. That was his alert, the one he used to warn me about legumes. "Don't start doing that all the time," I told him. "It'll get confusing."

He whined, and then seemed to sag with disappointment as he turned and trotted out to his usual sleeping place. I glanced at the offending corner once more, and then took myself to bed. Whatever bothered him in this room wasn't something I could fix tonight.

Chapter Ten

Monday was much more typical of a coastal Northern California day, and Taco seemed intent on making sure I was up to witness it. He was back in my room at dawn, whining at the corner of my room he hated.

"Taco, seriously," I groaned. I pulled my phone close to check the time. Without my contacts in or my glasses on, I could only read the screen if it was inches from my face. The news when I did so was not good. "It's not even six, pal." I rubbed my eyes and sat up, watching with annoyed fascination as my intelligent dog continued to be irritated by one corner of my bedroom.

"It's getting kind of old, Taco," I told him, but I pulled on my glasses and climbed out of bed, switching on the light to help him see the offending space more clearly.

Taco watched me, lying on the floor with both paws

close to the corner and his head turned. As I stepped near, he scooted over, as if giving me access to sniff the floor where he had. At a loss for anything else to do, I got down on my hands and knees and sniffed.

"I don't smell anything," I told him.

Taco whined.

"What do you want me to do, pull up the carpet?" I asked him. Daisy's bedroom—now my bedroom—was carpeted in a soft light blue pile that looked expensive. I really didn't want to start pulling it up just because my dog was going bananas for no reason, but I couldn't help the feeling I was beginning to have that Taco really needed to tell me something.

"Hang on," I told him, leaving the room to retrieve the stiff metal letter opener from the registration desk out front. Luckily, it was too early for guests to be meandering about the lobby, so no one witnessed me in my pajamas, which were covered with cartoon tacos.

"Okay, move," I suggested, returning with the pointy metal tool. I knelt again and wedged it into the space between the bottom of the moulding and the carpet, and pulled. Surprisingly, the carpet gave easily, as if the tack strips had already been detached. The entire corner pulled up along with the carpet padding below it, and revealed a planked wooden floor. "Who would cover this up?" I wondered aloud, but I knew that in the seventies and eighties, wall-to-wall carpet had been very in fashion.

Taco whined and crawled just a bit closer, nosing at the pulled-back carpet eagerly.

"This is really getting to you, huh?" I asked him. I tried wedging the letter opener between a few of the planks, but nothing felt loose or wiggly. I pulled the carpet back a little more and tried one more plank, which popped up when I pried beneath it.

"Oh!" I dropped it again, surprised, and then pulled it back up, more purposefully. When the plank was removed, I could see a hollow space below the floor, and in the darkened space, a box. "Oh hello," I whispered.

The box was about the size of a Kleenex box—the cube kind. I reached a hand down and pulled it up, and I had a sensation I imagined treasure hunters and intrepid historians must experience when they found something they'd been seeking.

What was this box? Had it been here for hundreds of years?

"How long does cardboard hold up?" I asked Taco, who didn't seem to know.

I put the box between us on the floor and Taco nosed it. Then he whined and let out three sharp barks. His alert.

"Is there something dangerous here?" I asked him. He only barked like that to warn me. And so far, he'd done it only about legumes.

I lifted the box's lid, and pulled it off to look inside.

"Well, that's the problem, isn't it?" I asked him. There

were peanuts in the box. A lot of them. Peanuts in their shells, acting almost like packing peanuts, because in the center was a small snow globe, which I removed. The snow globe had a lighthouse in the center of it, and a sign in front of the lighthouse that read "Salty Shores Lighthouse."

I shook the globe and watched the glittery snow fall around the little red and white striped structure. Taco watched me uneasily, his nose still twitching a hundred miles an hour. He was probably worried I might decide to eat the peanuts.

"Who would put a snow globe in a box and hide it?" I asked him, but Taco didn't answer. I dumped out the box, scattering peanuts over the carpet, much to Taco's consternation. A little folded square of paper slid out of the bottom of the box.

Was this Daisy's box? Had she left it for me? I'd emailed her once about Taco and the service he performed for me, but she'd never responded. Could she have hoped that a legume-sniffing dog would discover her hidden snow globe? But why on earth would my sister hide a child's souvenir?

I unfolded the little piece of paper. It was no more than a scrap, with a set of numbers scrawled on it in my sister's looping writing. The note read: "1, 6, 5, 3, 6, 12, 6, 5."

I assumed my sister had wanted me to find these things. The peanuts were obviously here to attract Taco's attention, and therefore mine. But why a game? It reminded me of the games Daisy and I had played as kids. We'd set up treasure hunts for one another and hidden things around Grandmother's farm. But would my sister really have been playing a game with me just before her death?

I didn't understand it, but sometimes my brain just took a little time to work things out. Right now, I needed to get the orange cranberry scones made for my guests, and then I hoped to hear from Owen about the coroner's report. And today I was resolved to start trying to find a gardener to take care of the inn's neglected garden.

I refolded the note, put it back into the box with the snow globe and set both on my dresser. Then I swept up the peanuts and threw them away, finally washing my hands well and then getting dressed.

"Now," I told Taco, "It's time to bake."

The scones were out, Diantha was at school, and things were just beginning to quiet down in the lobby when Mrs. Scolati came down the stairs holding Muffy.

"Dahlia, I'm glad you're here," she said, sounding breathless. "Your suggestion yesterday was a good one."

I had to think for a moment to remember what I'd suggested, exactly.

"The psychic. The dog psychic?"

"Oh yes," I said. "What did he tell you?"

Mrs. Scolati's face took on a grave expression. "Muffy has been communicating with a spirit. Here. At the inn."

I swallowed hard. I did not especially want to talk more about our resident ghost, so I tried to look as if I had no idea what she might be talking about.

"The inn is haunted. Did you not know that?" Her words were almost accusing, but her tone was not.

"No," I said, waiting to see what else she might add.

"Well, dogs are sensitive to these things, and Muffy has been bothered by a spirit in our room. She doesn't like the bathroom, especially."

"How interesting."

"I wanted to let you know, because of course you'll want to do something about that right away."

"Of course." I did not want to deal with Mr. Brown today. Or really at all. Since I didn't believe he existed. I hoped she wasn't going to insist.

"I actually think it's fascinating," Mrs. Scolati went on. "I'm a historian, you know. I have studied a lot of hauntings."

"Really?" That was an unexpected revelation.

"Oh yes. If you ever want to dig into the origins of your ghost and learn the right way to get rid of it... I might be able to help. Of course a responsible inn owner would handle it sooner rather than later."

I nodded, glad the Scolatis were checking out today. "I'll keep that in mind."

"Anyway, thank you. I also learned that Muffy doesn't enjoy salmon. It gives her heartburn."

"Good to know."

She nodded and then moved off toward the buffet, and Amal and I finally had time to discuss the garden out front.

"It's definitely not looking its best," she said when I brought it up.

"Okay, next question. Where do we find a gardener?"

Amal smiled. "I don't know. Internet? Library?"

"The library?"

"There's a bulletin board where people put up ads for services."

"I've seen those," I said, thinking aloud. The things with the little tabs at the bottom where you can pull off a phone number. "Yes, that's a good idea."

"Want me to swing by and check later?" Amal asked.

"Actually, I kind of need to go to the library anyway," I said, thinking there was a chance Daisy's numbers were the Dewey decimal code for a book. "Do you know, by any chance, did Daisy frequent the library?"

Amal's eyes narrowed slightly as if this question took her by surprise. "Now and then, I suppose. Especially when Danny was small."

I nodded. That made sense. "Do you know..." the question was forming before I really knew what I wanted to ask. "Did she ever talk about a lighthouse? Or a snow globe collection? Or peanuts?"

"Dahlia, are you feeling okay?" Amal shook her head lightly with a laugh. "Are those things related?"

"Sorry, no." Of course none of that made any sense. Amal didn't know about the box.

"There is a lighthouse," she said. "Springy shores or something. It's not in use anymore, but it's kind of a community landmark just up the coast."

"Salty shores?"

She laughed. "Yes, that's it."

"Did Daisy go there a lot?"

Amal leaned against the registration counter and tilted her head at me. "Not that I know about," she said slowly. "I think she took me there once to hike one of the trails that begins right there, though."

"Okay, thanks." I turned and busied myself tidying up the buffet, wrapping the remaining scones in plastic. I didn't want to tell Amal about the box I'd found, but I wasn't sure exactly why. When I felt like her attention had returned to the computer screen in front of her, I relaxed a little bit.

"Have you heard anything from Owen today?" Amal asked, reminding me that there were other things I was supposed to be thinking about besides the strange hidden box in my bedroom.

"Not yet," I said. "I'm expecting we'll hear about the coroner's report, if Owen is willing to share the findings with me."

"He will," she said. "Owen seems eager to share a lot of things with you." Her eyebrows wiggled in a suggestive way, and I felt the blush climbing my face again.

"I think I'll head to the library," I told Amal. "Just gonna get one thing inside first."

She nodded as Taco sprang to his feet, following me as I headed inside to grab the note. Then he trotted along next to me as I scooped up my sunhat and his leash. "See you in a bit."

The library was a partial win. I found a flyer advertising gardening services at what seemed a reasonable price from someone named Marcus. But I was not able to make Daisy's numbers even partially relate to the Dewey decimal numbers used for shelving books. It had been a long shot anyway.

Back at the inn, I produced the little scrap of paper I'd collected from the bottom of a flyer on the bulletin board. "There was one gardener flyer," I told Amal, handing her the number.

"Would you like me to call him?"

"Yes please."

She made a face at me, her lips turning down and her eyes rolling slightly.

"I'm terrible on the phone, Amal."

"You're fine on the phone."

I shrugged. The truth was that I didn't want to talk on the phone. I wanted to stew over the meaning of the note my sister had left me, but that was not to be. My cell phone rang just as I unleashed Taco, and I answered the call. It was Owen—I was happier to talk to him than to a stranger named Marcus.

"Hello," I said, trying not to sound too eager.

"Dahlia, hi." Even his voice held a smile.

"How are things going? Any new news on Mrs. Withers?"

"The coroner asked for one more day. I should have some information tomorrow. I did speak to the janitor again though. Strange fellow."

I didn't find Angus strange at all. "What do you mean?"

"I didn't go to him, he came here. He showed up today, asking to talk to me. He was very nervous, fidgeting and refusing to make eye contact through the whole interview."

"A lot of people find it very nerve wracking talking to the police, you know," I reminded him.

"Yes, but this seemed excessive. I'm starting to think he was involved. He wanted to know what kinds of things we'd found, what we believed happened."

"I'm nervous whenever I talk to anyone. And curious about investigations. It doesn't mean I committed a crime," I said.

"True," he responded.

I didn't know why I felt the need to defend the janitor —he'd had every reason to hate Mrs. Withers. She was mean to him. I just didn't see the guy killing anyone. But I didn't know him well, that was certain.

"Well, let me know if you find anything else you can tell me," I said.

"I'm kind of expecting you're going to find something to tell me instead," he laughed.

Solve one murder, and suddenly everyone expects you to solve them all.

I hung up with Owen, and found Amal giving me a squinty-eyed look from the registration desk.

"What?"

"You were talking on the phone. You know that, right?"

I laughed. "Yes, but Owen doesn't count. Did you talk to the gardener?"

"He's on his way over now. You're meeting him out front."

"I am?"

"You didn't want to talk on the phone, so you get to talk in person."

"Oh." Fair was fair, I supposed. "Right now?"

"Yep."

"Come on, Taco." I leashed my dog again and headed out front to meet Marcus, the gardener.

Chapter Eleven

"Allo there!" Just as I stepped outside, a white-haired man no taller than Diantha appeared around the corner, wearing overalls and a tool belt that held spades and cutters instead of hammers and screwdrivers. There was no question that this was the gardener.

"Marcus?" I asked, extending a hand to shake.

He took it gently and smiled, an expression that caused his bright blue eyes to sparkle from the deep wrinkles in his face. "That's me."

"I'm Dahlia, the owner of the inn."

"Ahh, yes. I'd heard something about it changing hands. Gorgeous place, Dahlia. And who's this?" Marcus leaned down to greet Taco, who I introduced. I wondered about him having known Daisy, or at least known about the inn, but I didn't know how to ask about that.

"Well, this is the garden, obviously. Shall we walk around a bit?"

"Let's do," Marcus said, his attention already pulled here and there by the various plants he saw. "Ah, someone has done a lovely job here," he said.

"My sister."

"Yes," he said thoughtfully. "Daisy, wasn't it? She had a knack." He bent to examine a low shrub, pushing the foliage this way and that.

"She did, yes. She's gone now, which is why I think we need some help."

Marcus straightened up and turned to me again, squinting at me in a way that made me feel like he was trying to decide what to say next. "I knew her a bit," he finally said. "Your sister. Nice lady."

"You met her?" I asked him.

He shook his head. "No, not really. Maybe bumped into her once or twice, heard nice things."

Marcus turned away, took a thick leaf between his fingers and leaned down to inspect it. When he rose, it was clear he had nothing more to say about my sister. "What are you looking for, Dahlia? Just maintenance? Or something more imaginative?"

I shook my head. "I really don't know. We just need to keep the garden looking nice for visitors," I explained.

"Course you do," he agreed. "And that's something I can do, certainly." Marcus's attention returned to the flowers at his feet, and he knelt down, pressing his fingers into the dirt and bending low. "Got a bit of irrigation in here, I see. Good, good."

"We do?" I didn't know there were any sprinklers in the garden.

"Just on the water-heavy plants. Most things get enough from the moisture in the air and the regular rain here," he told me.

"Ah, okay. Can you tell me a bit about your gardening experience?" I asked. I'd never interviewed a gardener, but had hoped for a resume at least. That was how things had worked when I'd been a defense contractor.

Marcus stood again, brushing his hands against the legs of his overalls. "Yup. Worked for twenty years at the university up the road. Retired, and now I just do odd jobs."

The university up the road could be Stanford, or UC Berkeley, or any number of other schools, big and small. I did think most universities had beautiful campuses, as a general rule. My mind conjured up expansive squares surrounded by lush greenery. Hopefully I wasn't wrong there.

"What was your position at the school?" I asked, searching for something clarifying like "head gardener."

Marcus seemed to find this very funny, and he guffawed for a minute and then caught my expression. "Oh, you're serious. Why, I was the gardener, Dahlia."

"Right," I agreed, feeling silly.

I didn't know what else to ask as Marcus looked at me expectantly. "Okay, well, why don't we start on a kind of trial basis? How many hours or days a week do you think you'll need to get this tidied back up?"

"I only work three days, and I'll have this place put back together by the end of the week. Two hours a morning."

"Okay," I said, about to ask about money.

"Thirty dollars an hour," he said. "Venmo."

"Ah, okay," I said. "I think that will work."

"Great," Marcus said, clapping his hands together. "I'll get started tomorrow."

"All right," I said. Taco pulled at the leash as Marcus made his way back to the front gate, trying to follow him. Taco seemed to like him, and that was usually a good sign.

I turned and went back inside.

"I hired a gardener," I told Amal. "He wants to be paid on Venmo."

"Great," she said, and then turned back to her computer screen.

Diantha arrived home from school almost as upset as she'd been that morning.

"Everyone is talking about Mrs. Withers," she said, flopping down in an overstuffed armchair. "About how she was murdered right there at school, at the bake sale with everyone around."

"We don't know that for sure," I reminded her, taking a seat on the ottoman as Taco dropped his head into her lap for patting.

"That's what they're saying," she moaned. "And some people are talking about how they aren't even sad she's gone."

"That's upsetting," I said, trying to figure out what needed saying in this situation. "Do you still feel like you're somehow responsible?"

Diantha sat up straight and stared at me. "I didn't push her off the cliff, Aunt Dolly. You were with me the whole time!"

"I'm not accusing you, Danny. Yesterday you felt worried that you weren't sad enough."

Diantha huffed out a breath. "I am sad, it's just..." she shook her head miserably. "I don't know how I feel. You just don't get it."

I wasn't even sure exactly what I didn't get, but I had no doubt she was right. "Maybe not. I do know that Owen is doing everything he can to find out what happened to Mrs. Withers."

She nodded sadly. I couldn't really understand her level of upset, given that Mrs. Withers was not a favorite teacher, and that Diantha had said some rather unkind things about her in the past. I did understand the idea that she might regret having said those things or thinking unkind thoughts, though. Maybe she needed a distraction.

"I wanted to show you something," I said, moving to pick my phone up off the front desk. "I worked up a pattern for the dog leashes that I think will work."

"I'm not doing them," she moaned, leaning back into the chair again.

"Well, I'm going to send this to you," I told her. "And if you change your mind and decide you'd like to work through one with me to get the hang of it, I'll be happy to help."

My niece did not answer, just began scrolling through her phone.

"Danny."

She looked up and I watched the annoyance in her features morph into something else as she looked at me. "I'm just tired, Aunt Dolly. Can I have a few minutes to zone out? Then maybe you can show me the pattern."

"Sure," I said, leaving her with Taco to "zone out."

Later that night, we did work through the pattern I'd created and Diantha made her first dog leash from the sturdy colorful twine I'd bought for the purpose.

"These are great!" she said, bouncing as she held her creation in her hands. "I'll show Tabitha after school tomorrow and see what she thinks."

"Perfect," I said, glad I'd managed to solve one problem today.

As I went to sleep, my mind worked through the strange Daisy-related events of the morning. First the box in the floor, and then the gardener's remarks.

When I finally drifted to sleep, I dreamt my sister was trapped in a lighthouse, calling to me.

Chapter Twelve

The morning came with news - a text from Owen.

Owen: Defensive bruising on Dorothy Withers's arms. Not consistent with an accident. Also, a broken hand.

Me: So... murder?

Owen: Looks like.

Me: Wow. Sorry. That's not good.

Owen: Understatement.

I put my phone down next to my coffee cup and stared absently out the big picture window on one side of the inn's lobby at the grey sky outside. But then the phone chimed again.

Owen: I have a feeling you'll be thinking about this, let me know if you come up with anything interesting.

Me: Sure.

I had no intention of digging any further into the

unfortunate death of Mrs. Withers. I wasn't a detective, and besides, I was starting to think I had a mystery of my own to solve. I hadn't slept well, my mind constantly returning to Daisy's strange note and to the lighthouse. More than that, I was suffering from guilt, wondering if it was fair for me to keep what I'd found from those who'd known Daisy best.

My desire to pursue answers around my sister would have to wait, though. I needed to go up to the school this morning to help Mr. Bentley finish the report for the bake sale earnings—something Dorothy would have done, but did not finish. For obvious reasons.

When Diantha appeared for breakfast, she looked a little bit less distressed than she had the night before.

"Sorry if I was weird yesterday, Aunt Dolly," she said, not meeting my eye as she shuffled her feet.

"It's okay, Danny. We're finding ourselves in some pretty unusual situations. They're tough to navigate."

She dropped to a squat and put her arms around Taco, who'd been sitting patiently in front of her, waiting for her to greet him. "Yeah," she said, her word muffled by his fur, where she'd planted her face.

"I'll drive you to school today," I told her. "I need to go speak to Mr. Bentley."

Diantha looked up at me then. "Are you going to solve the murder?"

I frowned at her. "No, I'm going to conclude my responsibilities to the bake sale."

"But you'll poke around while you're there, right?"

I shook my head. "Danny, I'm not an investigator. I'm an innkeeper. And a...guardian."

My niece made a face that told me she wasn't impressed with my answer. She was about to rise, to help herself to some of the egg bites steaming on the buffet, but I stopped her with a word.

"Danny?"

She turned back around, her eyebrows climbing up.

"Did you and your mom ever visit the Salty Shores Lighthouse?"

Diantha's eyes narrowed. "A couple times, why?"

"What did you do when you were there?"

"Lighthouse stuff. The first time I think we went in—I was really small. But then later, it was closed and we'd just go walk around. Sometimes Mom liked to just sit in the car and watch the sun set behind it."

"She took you to the lighthouse to sit in the car and watch the sun set?"

"It sounds weird when you say it like that."

"I just say it because you can watch the sun set from the patio here at the inn." Daisy had liked lighthouses when we were young... was that the entire connection? Why did I feel like there had to be something deeper?

Diantha lifted a shoulder. "Mom liked that lighthouse."

I guessed so. "Okay. Get something to eat. We'll go in twenty minutes."

A half hour later I sat across from Mr. Bentley in his office, receipts from the sales at the festival bake sale in a pile on his desk.

"I'm sorry to drag you in here," he said. His voice sounded normal, but his mouth didn't quite move normally as he spoke. I watched as he continued, wondering why I'd never noticed it before. "But with Dorothy gone, there are just some loose ends to tie up."

"It's no problem," I said, trying not to stare as he appeared to try to speak like a ventriloquist. Instead, I distracted myself looking around his office at the odds and ends he had on shelves and counter tops. There was a diploma from UC Davis, and a graduate degree from Berkeley. On a shelf near the degrees were a few photos—children, older people, and one where it looked like Mr. Bentley had cloned himself. "Mr. Bentley... are you a twin?"

Mr. Bentley stiffened for a moment and then followed

my gaze to the photo. "Oh, yeah. I am. That's my brother Tate."

"Identical?"

"Just about, yeah." He chuckled and then put a hand to his jaw.

"Does he live here?"

Principal Bentley dropped my gaze for a moment, then said, "Yes, he lives in town now." I had impression that there was something he wasn't saying, though it wasn't like I went around telling people all about my relationship with Daisy, either. Twin relationships could be hard. But then he added, "when we were kids, people confused us all the time."

"I am a twin too," I said, the words tinged with more sadness than I would have liked.

Mr. Bentley considered this, and then his face cleared with understanding. "Ah, Danny's mother."

I nodded. "We weren't identical, though. We always wanted to be. Especially after we saw 'The Parent Trap.'"

Principal Bentley smiled sadly. "I'm so sorry," he said, and for a moment a rush of emotion swept through me and I had a horrible feeling I might cry. I was able to swallow down the feeling, though. To cover what I feared might be written all over my face, I rose and moved to look at the photo more closely.

The two men were nearly identical, but Tate's part was on the opposite side to the principal's, and there was something different about his face, as if he spent less time smiling. I was willing to bet their mother relied on those small details to tell her boys apart. Cowlicks came in handy that way, I supposed.

When I'd managed to get my emotions in check, I turned and went back to my seat across from Principal Bentley.

"No service dog today, Dahlia?" he asked.

"I left him at the inn. I figured there was little chance we'd be eating anything."

"Ah," Principal Bentley smiled, the expression a little lopsided. "Well, shall we?"

I agreed, and together, we worked through the receipts and the hand accounting of each sale collected from the tables scattered around the bake sale. The numbers didn't match exactly, which troubled me. We were missing a couple hundred dollars.

"That's not good," I said, ready to begin again and see where we'd made an error.

"Oh, it's always a little off," Principal Bentley said. "With so many people involved, there's bound to be a margin of error. People give things away, forget to hand out the tickets customers take to the register, things like that."

I frowned at him. "I could understand twenty dollars, or maybe even fifty," I said. "But this is a large discrepancy. What if someone wasn't honest?"

"The parents at the Saltcliff School are upstanding

members of this community." He took an indignant tone, and I felt myself shrink as he continued. "I certainly wouldn't be accusing anyone of stealing. This is an honest error, I'm sure. It happens every year."

Well. I didn't say it, but I thought that if I was running an event that came out several hundred dollars short of where it should each year, I'd be revamping my systems to be more efficient. I couldn't imagine Dorothy Withers would accept this answer.

"Okay," I said after a moment. It wasn't my place to argue, even if I didn't like it.

"I think that's all we need then," Principal Bentley said, rising. "Thank you for your time and for organizing everything at the sale."

I nodded, rising across from him. "I'm sorry things didn't go smoothly. With Mrs. Withers..."

Mr. Bentley made a face, his mouth turning down and his eyes narrowing. "Nasty business."

It was. And when I left his office, I couldn't help but be drawn to the edge of the parking lot, to the path that led down to the cove where Mrs. Withers had died.

The tide was out, so I walked carefully down the path, using the handrail that had been placed in certain spots to secure my stability as I descended. It was a steep path, but not as treacherous as I'd imagined. The path twisted along the side of the rugged cliff as it led down to the sandy beach at the bottom.

I stepped out onto the sand, looking at the jagged dark rocks along one side of the beach with new appreciation. It would be possible to fall on those rocks from the path above, or to loose one's footing if you were to climb out onto them for a better view of the ocean. What in the world had Dorothy Withers been doing down here the day of the festival?

I wandered the sandy edge of the cove, my eyes scanning for anything that might help me understand her intentions, but of course, there was nothing the police hadn't already found. I wasn't eager to climb up onto the rocks where Mrs. Withers had breathed her last, even though they'd been washed clean several times by the incoming tide since her death.

For a few moments, I stood still, gazing out at the rolling waves crashing over those treacherous rocks. It was mesmerizing, almost hypnotic. But my trance was broken when one wave came closer than I'd expected, soaking me in sea spray as it smashed into the rocks. The tide was coming in. Quickly.

I turned, heading back for the bottom of the path, shocked at the way the water seemed to chase me. Each wave broke closer and closer to the cliff wall behind me, and I realized that the tides were shifting, and that in a few minutes, this cove would be underwater, with the possible exception of the jagged rocks where Dorothy Withers had been found.

I reached the path and the railing, and climbed, watching below me as the ocean reclaimed the cove. I'd escaped, but my shoes bore the marks of sand and surf, and the salt had left a line around the tops of the soles. I wondered if it would wash out.

Finally, I was back in my sister's car, heading back to the inn to check on Marcus, my head full of questions about Dorothy Withers, the principal's acceptance of poor accounting practices, and ocean tides.

Chapter Thirteen

I arrived back at the inn to find Marcus on his knees out front, a mounting pile of weeds beside him.

"I guess the garden has been neglected a little too long," I said, feeling oddly guilty for having let things get out of hand.

Marcus sat back on his heels and smiled up at me. "Nothing I can't handle. Your sister did some smart planting in here. A lot of things she put together repel weeds and insects naturally."

"Oh. Good." It felt like Daisy was on my mind more than ever, like she was taking up residence in a bigger and bigger part of my brain while I simultaneously took up more and more of her previous life.

I stood awkwardly beside the old man for a moment, feeling unsure how to behave. I wasn't used to people doing work I could easily be doing myself, but I was paying him to garden, so offering to help would be odd.

"You've lived in this area a while?" I asked, deciding that just getting to know the man a bit might be the right answer.

"All my life, ma'am," he said, sitting back up again on his heels. He had a padded cushion beneath his knees, I saw now. It made me feel better about him working out here on the hard path for some reason. "Seen this place change from little known wilderness to tourist paradise in my years." He nodded, and his eyes took on a faraway look. "You know, people didn't used to take this landscape for granted the way we do now."

"What do you mean?"

"When the first artists moved into this area, it was cheap property. Overgrown, thick and dense. They had their work cut out for them, trying to clear enough space to put up cottages and actually live here." He nodded, seemingly to himself. "Those rocks out there?" He pointed to the cliffs. "Kept boats from landing or even getting close. There's no marina or yacht club for the rich folks because it's so dangerous."

That made sense. My mind flashed to the lighthouse, which must have been built to keep boats well aware of this treacherous coastline.

"We've tamed this little spit of land now," Marcus went on. "But it's still wild at heart. If we all left her alone for fifty years, she'd reclaim this land. All the fancy shops and restaurants would get retaken by Mother Nature. Garden here's proof enough of that."

"I... oh," I said, unsure how to answer. Marcus had become more animated as he finished his history lesson, and I sensed he wasn't a big fan of tourism in general. "Marcus," I asked. "Do you know when the Salty Shores Lighthouse stopped operating?"

"Years ago," he said. "You know they used that place for secret meetings during Prohibition?"

"They did?" So it had been shut down since the twenties, at least.

"It's always been a bit of a draw for nefarious types trying to operate under the radar."

"And a tourist attraction, right?"

"For a little while, I guess. I suspect that was more about the Mariners trying to make things look on the up and up for a bit. Get right with law enforcement and what not."

"The Mariners?" I asked. "The baseball team?"

That made Marcus laugh, a hearty rumbling sound that turned his cheeks pink beneath the floppy sun hat he wore. "No ma'am. The crime syndicate."

"Crime syndicate?"

"Ah, well, don't you worry about them. Just keep your nose clean and if anyone makes you an offer that sounds too good to be true, you just walk the other way."

"I'm sorry, I'm not sure I understand."

Marcus glanced around guiltily, and then leaned forward again, back at his task. "I'm not really at liberty to say more, ma'am. I'll just get on with it."

"Oh." Well that was interesting. "Okay, thanks, Marcus." I went inside and was going to ask Amal what she knew about the Mariners, but that would have to wait. There was chaos in the lobby of the inn.

"You know very well that Julia is my best friend from college. But I've known *Julie* since elementary school. Julia lives here, and that's part of why we came to visit. *Julie* lives in Saskatchewan now. She's turned to a life of solitude, living off the land and weaving ladies undergarments out of hemp, but that's a whole other thing." Mrs. Crawford stood in the center of the inn's usually cozy and quiet lobby, shouting these words at her husband, Vance Crawford, who stood on the other side of the room.

"How the heck am I supposed to keep all your kooky friends straight?" he hollered back. "You pick up people like most people gather spare change, and every single one of them is weird and has the same danged name."

"The weirdness should make them easier to remember," Mrs. Crawford yelled back.

Amal stepped quickly to my side as I entered. "This has been going on for ten minutes now."

I stared at the couple, engaged in some kind of socially related standoff, and at the rest of the guests cowering on furniture scattered between them. Taco had crawled under the coffee table and put his paws over his head. Even my pathologically empathetic dog had given up on calming this down. "How did it start?"

"They were sitting at the table eating, and all of a sudden, this happened." Amal looked irritated, tucking one piece of hair behind her ear. "I asked them to quiet down, and they ignored me."

"Julie, Julia, Julianne, Julian," Mr. Crawford said, counting on his fingers. "No sane person on earth could keep it all straight."

"I can't help that I have an affinity for J people," Mrs. Crawford sniffed. "It has to do with my chakras."

I stepped close to her side. "Good morning, Mrs. Crawford," I said.

She glanced at me, and then yelled back at her husband. "It's better than your friends. Frank and Gene and Howard. All you guys ever do is sit around and drink beer and watch football."

"It's called relaxing," he shouted back. "And my friends all have different names. It's like you're making the same friend over and over. Branch out a little, will ya?"

"I wondered," I continued, "If I might encourage you to take this out onto the back patio?"

Shirley Crawford turned to face me. "Take what? Breakfast?"

"The, ah... the yelling." Discomfort swam in my stomach, and I had a momentary longing for my old life, my silent apartment. The thought receded as I glanced at Amal again though. This was better. If a bit louder and less predictable.

"We're not yelling," she told me before yelling back at her husband. "You're impossible!"

"Have you seen the garden?" I asked, feeling desperate as other guests were gathering food onto little plates and heading for the stairs. "There is a rose out there called a Juliette rose. Maybe with your affinity for J things, you'd enjoy having some cuttings in your room?"

"You can send those up later," she told me, waving me away. She opened her mouth again, presumably to scream something else about her social sphere at her husband, when the inn's door opened again and a woman stepped in.

"Shirley!" The woman cried upon seeing Mrs. Crawford.

"Julia!" Mrs. Crawford turned and hugged the woman. Her husband rolled his eyes, sighed loudly and dropped into a chair by the fire, picking up his phone.

"I'm so glad you called me while you're here in town. You have got to come hiking today along the cliffs. So pretty." Julia glanced around the lobby. "Oh, this place is so cozy."

I lingered, feeling out of place in my own home suddenly.

"Vance, are you ready to go?" Mrs. Crawford called to

her husband, her voice suddenly sweet. "Julia is here to pick us up."

Vance Crawford didn't say a word until he was inches from his wife, and then in a friendly voice, he said, "So nice to see you again, Julia. Thanks for sharing some time with us."

"Of course!" Julia cried, and soon, the threesome was out the door and the lobby was peaceful again. Taco climbed out from below the table and came to my side, pushing his big head against my thigh as if seeking comfort.

"It's okay, buddy," I told him. "They're done yelling."

"That was..." Amal shook her head as she met my eyes.

"Yeah. Very..." I tried to find a word to describe what we'd just witnessed, but only laughter erupted from my chest.

Soon, Amal and I were both laughing hard, shaking our heads. I put one hand on the edge of the desk for balance and Amal wiped at her eyes.

Some of the other guests were wearing relieved smiles or chuckling now too.

"What in the world?" I asked Amal, finally recovering from the laughing fit.

"I have no idea. They just kind of erupted into it."

"What a strange argument."

"The strangest thing was that neither of them seemed really upset, or to notice that there were other people around getting extremely uncomfortable," Amal said.

"Maybe they always communicate like that," I guessed.

"We need to add a new question to the intake form for guests."

"Right. 'Do you enjoy screaming arguments about ridiculous topics in public venues?'" I suggested.

"I'll get right on that."

For a few minutes, I tidied the lobby and cleaned up the remains of breakfast. When things were mostly in order and most of the guests had moved on with their days, I went back to the desk where Amal was working.

"I spoke to Owen," I told her. "The coroner says Mrs. Withers had defensive bruising on her arms, a broken hand, and that her head injury wasn't from a fall on the rocks. She fought with someone and was hit with something heavy—a rock, she suggested."

"Oh no," Amal said, her face pulling into a frown. "Who would want to kill Dorothy Withers?"

"I don't know. The janitor certainly didn't like her, and you heard Mr. Franklin at the bake sale. She had a way of making parents angry too. I'm not sure who would have taken things to that level, but I suppose we're going to find out soon." I was about to head inside to start working on the baking for tomorrow, when I remembered what I'd been about to ask Amal about in the first place. "Amal, have you ever heard of a group called the Mariners?"

She lowered her brows and pressed her lips together in a twisted little smile. "Big guys? Carry bats?"

"Uh, bats? And maybe guns, I guess," I said, trying to imagine what members of a crime syndicate might look like.

"Guns? For baseball?"

A laugh escaped me again, realizing Amal had made the same error I had. "Oh, sorry. Not baseball. I guess it's a crime syndicate."

She dropped my gaze and I suddenly suspected that Amal knew more about the Mariners than she'd wanted me to believe.

"Amal?"

My friend lifted her gaze again and looked around, as if someone might be listening to us. "Whatever you're digging into there, it'd be best to leave it alone."

Chapter Fourteen

I spent Wednesday working around the inn, turning over a few rooms—the screaming couple checked out early in the morning and I found myself relieved. Screaming made me anxious.

As I worked, changing linens, dusting surfaces and restocking things in each guest room, my mind moved as if detached from the rest of me.

It was easy to appreciate my surroundings while I puttered around the cozy guest rooms we rented to visitors. Each one was named for one of Daisy's favorite literary characters, though she didn't go so far as to decorate in theme. Instead, each room had a kind of modern farmhouse feel, with overstuffed furniture, whitewashed wood, and soft blues on the walls and linens. The rooms on the back of the inn had a gorgeous view of the Pacific Ocean, and most had chairs set up with a little table between them so guests could sit and watch the ocean, or see the sun set right out their windows.

Most of the bathrooms had been remodeled at some point recently, because the fixtures were sleek and modern without being at odds with the cottage feel of the rest of the inn. We had two more to do, but Amal and I hadn't set a budget and timeline for that project quite yet.

As I finished making the last bed in the Gatsby Suite, my mind had turned to Mrs. Withers and the sad events of the bake sale.

The thing that still wasn't sitting right—beyond the fact that Mrs. Withers had been murdered in the first place —was the principal's easy dismissal of several hundred dollars missing from the sale's proceeds. I knew it wasn't kind to suspect the dead of misdoings, but could Mrs. Withers have been skimming off the top for years? The principal asserted that the sale was always short.

It seemed unlikely, but once I'd gotten the idea that she might have at least known something about the mismanaged money, I couldn't let it go.

Dorothy Withers was a meticulous woman... would she have kept some kind of personal records? And could I find a way to get a look at them?

When I'd finished loading the last set of sheets into the laundry down in the basement of the inn—interestingly, the inn had a basement separate from that of our little apartment—I made a quick phone call.

"Saltcliff School, this is Rosamund. How can I help you?"

I remembered Rosamund. I wondered if my cookies had maybe earned me a bit of goodwill with the secretary. "Hello Rosamund. This is Dahlia Vale, Diantha's guardian?"

"Of course, Dahlia, how are you?"

"I'm doing well, thank you, I—"

"Can you believe Mrs. Withers was murdered? At the bake sale?" This was uttered in a harsh whisper, and I could picture the secretary turning with the phone and hunching so as not to be heard by any other staff or students nearby.

"It's really terrible," I said.

"It would almost be sad if she wasn't such a horrible person."

Oh. "Well, right. Yes." I wondered if Rosamund had any sort of motive. She was clear about her dislike for Dorothy. I made a mental note to mention it to Owen when I spoke to him next. "How can I help you, Dahlia?"

"Two things," I said, hoping I'd get away with what I was planning. "First, can you let Diantha know I'll be picking her up today? She won't need to walk home."

"Oh sure. Sweet girl, Danny."

"She is," I agreed.

"What else can I do for you?"

I needed to tell a little lie, something I was inherently

terrible at. Logic was my friend, and I had a bad habit of taking and putting things quite literally in general. Lies were, at their core, the complete opposite. "I think I left some papers in Mrs. Withers's classroom when I visited her there. I wondered if it would be too much trouble for me to go see if I can retrieve them."

"Oh," Rosamund hesitated. "Well, they've kind of just kept her room locked up since... everything."

"Of course."

"But if you were to just be in and out, I'm sure it would be okay," she said. "I can ask Angus to meet you there to open the door."

"That would be great," I said. I glanced at the lobby clock, which let me know that Diantha would be getting out of school in just over an hour. "Could I head over now?"

"Sure, just pop into the office to let us know you're here."

Fifteen minutes later, I was at the school, standing outside the classroom where I'd first met Dorothy Withers, with the man she'd yelled at that first day.

"Thank you for this, Angus."

Angus unlocked the classroom door and then stepped inside with me, closing it behind him. "It's a terrible thing," he said, rubbing a hand over the back of his neck. "Terrible."

"It is," I agreed, his behavior catching my attention. I

studied him as he shifted his weight back and forth staring at the floor. He seemed extremely uncomfortable. I wondered if it was just being in a dead woman's classroom that was getting to him. "Are you all right, Angus?"

He looked up at me then, a searching stare, as if he was trying to discover something in my face. "I don't know, ma'am. I just really don't know."

I shook my head. What? What did that mean? "Um. Is there something I can do?"

Angus stared at me a beat longer, making me begin to fidget with the handle of Taco's leash. Taco seemed completely unfazed by the janitor's odd behavior, throwing himself down in a heap at my feet. He seemed to have decided that if we weren't moving, he might as well sneak in a quick nap. He let out a little groan as he rolled to his side.

"I didn't like her," he said, his raspy voice nearly a whisper. "But I didn't want her to die, either."

"Of course not," I said. "Everyone knows that."

"That policeman seemed pretty suspicious."

I remembered Owen's assessment of the janitor. Could he have killed Dorothy? Looking at the worried man before me, I supposed it was possible.

"Angus, do you know anything about why Dorothy went down to the cove?"

His chin shot up and he held my eyes for a long beat. "No," he said finally. Then he turned and headed for the door. "I'll be working on the grounds just outside. You tell me when you're finished in here."

A moment later, I was alone in Dorothy's classroom.

"Okay, Taco. Let's have a look around."

Taco lifted his head to look at me, but then seemed to decide my suggestion was merely rhetorical. He lowered his head again, and let out a long breath.

"Okay then. I'll have a look around." I dropped his leash to the floor beside him and went to the big desk in the front of the room. I wanted to see if Mrs. Withers had any records from previous bake sales. She'd been running it for years, so if there was always a financial discrepancy, certainly she'd have noted that somewhere?

I opened the top drawer in her desk, but found nothing there beyond a few tubes of ChapStik, some Post-Its and pens, and some loose change.

The drawer on the right contained a lunch bag that I hoped was empty, and the one on the left held file folders labeled alphabetically with what I assumed were student's names. I restrained myself when I saw one labeled "Vale." This was not what I'd come for. I pushed the drawer shut and rose, looking around the room.

"There." In the back of the room against the far wall was a filing cabinet, the big kind with two long drawers. When I pulled the top drawer open, I struck gold. There was a hanging folder labeled "Bake Sale 2023" and another one for each of the previous years, all the way back to the year 2014. I pulled the previous year's records and spread the folder open on the counter at the side of the room.

There was a map, like the one Dorothy had given me. There were lists of donations and names of participants, and there at the back was a balance sheet, showing the money generated by the sale.

I assumed that the numbers in the two rows labeled "goods sold total" and "money submitted" would be identical, but they were nearly three hundred dollars off. The same was true for each of the previous years, going back to 2010. In that year, the lines matched perfectly, as did all the sales prior.

"That's odd." I said. I wondered if the other money-generating portions of the Saltcliff Festival also had discrepancies. I decided to check in with Principal Bentley to find out, and to let him know what I'd found.

I gathered the folders and retrieved Taco's leash, turning off the light as I stepped out the door to look for Angus.

"Oh!" I didn't need to look for him. He was standing right next to the door, and he startled me as I emerged.

"Sorry, Ms. Vale."

"That's okay," I said, recovering myself. "I'm all done," I told him. "I'm just going to take these things back to the office for the principal."

He nodded and locked up the room, but before I could

head for the office, Angus said, "I might know why Mrs. Withers went to the cove." His voice was nearly a whisper and I wasn't sure I had heard him right. I turned to face him fully.

"What?"

"I know why she went down there."

"You do?"

Angus's face was a mask of misery, his eyes filled with tears and his cheeks red. "It was my fault," he said, his voice a low wail. "But I was only trying to scare her. I told her there were kids down there vandalizing the cove. And I knew the tide was coming in. She was so mean to everyone, nothing was ever good enough for her. She made everyone's life so miserable."

"Angus," I said slowly, feeling like a very delicate moment was hanging in the balance. "Did you tell the detective this?"

Angus shook his shaggy head. "I was scared," he said. "But I'm ready now. I didn't mean to, but I think I killed Mrs. Withers."

I hadn't even been asked to help with this investigation, and I had gotten a confession. Shock trickled through me. What did I do now?

The janitor looked so forlorn I was tempted to tell him it was okay. But this was a murder—intentional or otherwise. Plus, Mrs. Withers had bruises on her arms, as if she fought someone off. How could it have been an accident?

None of this was for me to figure out. "We'll need to call Owen," I told Angus.

He stared at the ground, but I discerned a tiny nod.

"Let's go to the office. We can do it there, and you can wait for him to arrive."

Another nod, and then Angus shuffled toward the office and I followed him, carrying my files and holding Taco's leash. We were just to the door when the bell chimed loudly through the corridor, and students began emerging from the doors along the hall.

Inside, I suggested Angus take a seat, and then put my files onto a chair next to him while I dug my cell phone from my bag. Taco sat next to Angus and dropped his furry head on the man's lap, clearly sensing the janitor's distress.

"Hey Dahlia," Owen answered after two rings.

"Owen, hello."

"Is everything all right?"

"Yes. Well, kind of. I'm at the school. With Angus, the janitor."

"Okay," Owen's drawn out word indicated that he knew there was more to it.

"He just told me he might know something about why Dorothy was in the cove." I swiveled away from Angus to whisper, "Owen, I think he confessed."

"Oh. Well, okay," he said, his voice taking on a more serious tone. "I'll be right over. Can you keep him in one place?"

I glanced at the man slumped in the chair. "We're in the office. I don't think he'll go anywhere.'

"I'll be right there." Owen hung up, and I turned back to Angus.

"The detective is on his way. Can you wait here?"

Angus didn't look up, just nodded. He seemed resigned to his fate, whatever it might be.

I stepped to the desk, where Rosamund was talking to a student. After a moment, the boy walked away and she smiled at me.

"Hi again," I said. "Is Principal Bentley available for a quick minute by any chance?"

"I can check," she said. "Uh, what's all this?" She angled her head at the poor janitor who was practically in tears at the side of the office space.

"He's waiting for Detective Sanderson. He shouldn't leave," I said. "Taco will watch him." My dog remained still, his head on the man's lap.

"Um, okay," Rosamund said, looking uncertain. She turned and lifted the receiver on the phone, and then turned back to me. "He says you can come right in."

I gathered the folder from the chair and said to Angus, "be right back. Stay here, okay?"

"Okay." It was clear he had no intention of going anywhere.

I headed for the principal's office and knocked lightly.

"Come on in, Dahlia," he called.

146

Inside the little office, there were folders piled here and there, and I resisted the urge to organize everything immediately. Instead, I added my stack of folders to the mess, finding a clear spot in the front of the principal's desk.

"What's all this?" he asked, his jaw operating more normally than the last time I'd seen him.

"I wanted to show you something," I said. "You mentioned that there'd been a discrepancy in the receipts every year the bake sale ran."

"Sure, sure," he said waving this off. "No big deal."

"Well, right, sir... except, there was never a discrepancy until 2013. And then it was the same amount of money missing every single year."

"Was it?" The principal was looking over a memo of some kind while I spoke.

"Three hundred and fifty dollars every year. Including this one," I pointed out.

"Well, that's not much money in the grand scheme of things, is it?"

I thought about that. "I guess it depends on your perspective. But over the last ten years, that becomes a big sum. And if every single sales location at the festival is reporting a similar loss..."

The principal said nothing, but I had his attention now.

"How many different registers operate during a regular festival?"

"We have between fifteen and twenty different vending locations," he said.

"If there were fifteen, and each lost three hundred and fifty dollars, that's a loss of over five thousand dollars this year alone," I pointed out. And over the past ten years, that amounts to just over fifty thousand dollars."

The principal said nothing, but his expression had hardened.

"Doesn't that worry you?" I pressed. "The school could certainly use that money, couldn't it?"

He rose now, and his voice was like steel. "Dahlia, it would be in everyone's best interest for you to let this go. Right now."

I stared at him. "So you did know?"

"I think you better leave," he told me. "And you don't want to mention this to anyone."

Was he threatening me? "But sir, there's—"

"This is serious," he said. "I'll handle it. But do not breathe a word to anyone. I'm warning you. For your own safety."

"Okay," I said slowly, getting to my feet.

"Thank you for your help. I've got it from here."

We stared at each other for another second, and then Rosamund's voice came over the little speaker on his desk.

"Principal Bentley? Diantha Vale is here for Dahlia. And uh... the police are here too."

"You called the police?" Principal Bentley practically hissed this at me.

I shook my head. "For a different matter."

He looked so angry, a spark of fear actually ignited inside me and I moved quickly to the door, pulling it open. Across the office, I found Owen's face, and the fear died immediately.

Diantha was holding Taco's leash, and I walked to where she stood, dropping an arm around her shoulder in a half-hug. I wasn't sure if it was me who really needed the contact—I wasn't traditionally a hugger—but the discussion with the principal had disturbed me.

"Good day?" I asked her.

"Pretty good," she said, her eyes on Owen as he talked in a low voice to Angus. "What's going on?"

"Let's head home. I'll tell you in the car." I was eager to get out of the building, away from the principal.

"Dahlia, thanks for the call," Owen said, seeing Dahlia and I waiting for his attention. "We'll talk later?"

I nodded and turned for the door.

"Bye Dahlia, by Danny!" Rosamund called. She, for one, seemed thrilled with all the excitement in the office that afternoon.

I hurried Taco and my niece to the little Fiat and pulled out of the parking lot, maybe a tad faster than I should have.

"Aunt Dolly, you're freaking me out."

I was a little freaked out too.

Chapter Fifteen

That night I couldn't sleep.

Owen hadn't checked in after he'd taken Angus in, and I imagined the kind janitor spending his night in a cold jail cell at the police station. Had he really killed Dorothy Withers? He'd all but admitted it.

Actually, he had admitted it. Though he'd said it was an accident. I just wasn't sure I could imagine it, but then murder wasn't something I'd had much experience with in general. Even the most gentle soul had a trigger that might turn us into a version of ourselves we didn't recognize.

Still, something didn't feel complete about Angus's confession, and I was eager to hear Owen's thoughts.

Until then, however, I had things to attend to.

"Ready, Taco?" I asked my dog once I'd dressed and given him breakfast. Most dogs liked to get out first thing in the morning and handle their business, but Taco was too focused on food. Once he'd demolished his breakfast, only then could he consider other matters. Now he looked up at me from his water dish with water dripping from his jowls, a smile in his soft amber eyes.

I clipped on his leash and we headed out the apartment door into the lobby and out the front door of the inn. It was early, which meant guests were still tucked up in their beds, though midweek we didn't have too many people to look after.

Taco and I wandered the garden, but saw no sign of Marcus quite yet besides the clear effects of his presence here, which came in the form of tidy paths and trimmed plants everywhere I looked.

"A quick stroll up Nutmeg," I suggested to Taco, who was eager to accompany me pretty much anywhere.

We turned out of the inn's gate and headed for the main street of town, which shone dark in the lingering dampness of morning. The fog hung over the low branches of the pines and eucalyptus trees, and I suppressed a shiver. Fall was undoubtedly here, and its arrival in town was marked along the sidewalk with Halloween and pumpkin-themed displays in store windows and next to shop doors.

As we walked, I planned my day.

Muffins first, and then I'd make a quick batch of egg bites to put out this morning.

There was one room to turn over, and I'd need to finish

up the laundry I'd begun the day before. Amal wanted to discuss the accounts and we'd agreed to see if we had enough on hand to renovate the bathroom in the Atticus suite before the holidays. I wanted to talk to Owen, but I imagined he'd check in with me when he had time—he knew I'd be curious. And my brain was still circling the strange encounter I'd had with the principal and the disparities in accounting that seemed to have plagued the festival for several years. And there was still the note and the snow globe.

Back at the inn, I finished up the baking as Diantha appeared, ready for school.

"Aunt Dolly?" She asked, looking uncertain in a way my brave niece rarely did lately.

I set down the pan I'd just emptied of egg bites and gave her my attention.

"Would it be okay if I went in Mom's room—er, uh, your room—and borrowed a necklace she had from her jewelry box?"

My heart twisted inside me at her uncertain tone.

"Of course," I said, and together, we headed to the bedroom at the back of the apartment.

Diantha paused in front of the dresser, where Daisy's jewelry box sat. I'd opened it, but I'd never really investigated the contents. As her fingers lifted the lid, Diantha's eyes slid to the other items on the dresser top, and landed on the snow globe.

"What's that?"

I batted down the sudden urge to snatch it up and hide it. Diantha might as well know what I'd found.

I explained where it had come from as Diantha turned the souvenir in her small hands.

"Can I see the note?"

I showed it to her, tugging it out of my phone case.

"Okay, that's confusing," she said, looking back at the plastic globe in her hands.

"So you don't know what it means either?" I asked.

She shook her head and then raised the snow globe, shaking it much harder in front of her than I'd done so far. Glitter scattered within the tiny world of the lighthouse, but something else happened that got my attention.

A little ding came from the globe, along with a second note.

"It's a music box!" Diantha said, shaking it again. But only one other lone note emanated from the globe, and her face fell a bit. She flipped it over in her hand, holding it, bottom-up, between us.

"There used to be a knob to wind it up, I think," I said, pointing to the little hole where a tiny metal prong could be see inside the casing.

"Oh, it's broken," Diantha said. "I wonder what it plays."

I shrugged, taking the globe as she handed it to me and turned her attention to the jewelry box. The piece she ended up extracting was a small golden bumble bee on a long decorative chain. "Think it would be okay if I wore this?" she asked.

"I think your mom would like that," I said.

We headed back into the kitchen, where I took a second tray of egg bites out of the oven and tipped them onto the plate with the others.

"Ohh, egg bites," Diantha said, snatching one off the plate I was about to carry out to the lobby.

"Careful, they're—"

"Oooh, hot, hot." She spit a bite of egg back into her palm.

"Hot. Yes."

"Sorry." My niece shot me a sheepish smile, and I got a quick glimpse of the goofy little girl she still was sometimes. Today she wore orange and black striped tights beneath her black, shapeless dress, and a beanie pulled over her head. She'd pulled back on the eye makeup, but it seemed like the only lipstick she had access to was in shades of black, dark blue, and purple.

I decided there were probably going to be more important battles to fight one day. I wasn't going to bother her about lipstick.

"Come eat in the lobby. Maybe have a glass of milk while you let these cool a bit."

"Good idea," she said, following me out the big door, Taco on our heels.

I arranged the food and tidied up a bit while Diantha ate, and Amal arrived, stashing her bag beneath the registration desk.

"So do you really think the janitor killed Mrs. Withers?" Diantha asked us both, coming to stand in front of the desk.

Amal shook her head slowly, and I shrugged. "I have no idea."

"He confessed, though," Amal said, recalling what I'd told her the night before.

"Kind of. He confessed to knowing why she was at the cove, and said he hadn't meant to kill her. I don't know if that's a full confession." I'd also told Amal about my odd interaction with Principal Bentley, but she'd suggested it might be smart to let the school finances rest with those working at the school.

Which was probably wise, but it still bothered me.

"A lot of the kids at school think Sam's dad killed Mrs. Withers," Diantha offered.

"Mr. Franklin?" I asked.

She nodded, pushing half a muffin into her mouth.

"He was angry about his son's grade, but that doesn't really seem like a motive," I mused.

"Parents around here are pretty serious about their kids' grades," Amal said. "They all compete starting in preschool to see who can get into the best colleges and programs. Same with sports—it's very brutal."

"That seems a bit over the top," I said, but I'd heard parents talking that way– about grades and sports competitions and travel teams and more.

"People lose sight of common sense where their children are concerned," she said.

"Plus," Diantha said, coming to stand in front of the desk. "I guess Sam's dad disappeared for like, the whole festival."

"I saw him there," I pointed out. "Assembling the big booth."

"And arguing with Dorothy Withers," Amal added.

"But that was just in the morning," Diantha said. "Did you see him later?"

Amal and I exchanged a look. "No," I admitted. "I'll make sure Owen considers him if he hasn't already."

Once Diantha had gone to school, I headed down to the basement laundry room to finish up the sheets I'd started the day before. The stairs led from a door next to the lobby bathroom down into the musty space, which was largely unfinished. It was cool and damp, and I didn't enjoy the environment at all, so hadn't spent much time here if I didn't have to. Now, though, I wandered the space as I set the dryer for one more speed cycle to freshen the sheets I'd let sit overnight.

The machines sat on one wall, with a tall rack for drying clothes that held detergent and other supplies on top.

The opposite wall was a few feet away, and the single fixture overhead did little to light that part of the space. There was one narrow window at the very top of the side wall, which was filmy and dirty, letting in the sparsest of dim light from outside.

As I stepped closer, I noticed an indentation in the wall, almost like a hole where a doorknob might be inserted. I traced it with my fingers, and felt the metal attachment just inside. It seemed there was a doorknob here, but it had been removed. On closer inspection, it was clear there was a door here, though the outline was nearly hidden in the rough texture of the concrete wall.

I tried slipping my fingers in and pulling it open, but the door was latched. I needed the knob. Curious, I bent down and tried to peer through the door, but couldn't see anything through the knob mechanism in the hole.

What was in the secret room? Was it actually a secret room?

I looked around the basement, becoming more curious by the moment. There were a few boxes scattered around, and I began taking the tops off, digging through holiday ornaments and linens stored in them. As I took a final box from the shelf next to the laundry, I got lucky. There was a knob rolling around inside. Could I just stick it in and hope it would work?

It did. I inserted the gold knob and turned, and the pin pulled open the latch, allowing me to push the door open into the hidden room. For a moment I just stood there, an eerie sense of foreboding washing through me. It felt like I'd just gained entry to a place I was never meant to see.

Did Amal know this was here? Had Daisy known?

I took a step inside, an uncomfortable fear rising within me. I was rarely afraid. It didn't make sense in most situations to be afraid. What could possibly hurt me here? A spider, maybe.

Still, I had the sense that I was not entirely alone as I leaned into the darkness beyond the door.

For a moment I stood still, holding my breath and listening. Only silence filled my ears, along with a faint dripping sound. Soon, my eyes were adjusting to the darkness, and I glanced around the space, finding an old push-button switch on the wall next to the door. As I depressed the button, a light overhead flickered on, and surprise and wonder filled me in equal measure.

The room appeared to be a small bar or club of sorts. There was a bar against one wall, shelves above it lined with dusty old bottles standing like neglected sentinels. The brass rail along the side of the bar wore a dark patina, but there were spots where it still shone. Several leather-topped stools stood in front of the bar, and the corners of the space were scattered with small round tables and low club chairs. A bookcase stood empty on the far wall.

Why was there a club under the inn?

I stepped in farther, noticing that the air was thick with

dust—how long had it been since anyone had disturbed this space? For a few moments, I toured around the room, my feet leaving prints in the thick dust on the floor. As I neared the far wall, I noticed a second door, this one on the wall that would connect into the basement of the apartment upstairs. The door was locked.

But in front of it were several footprints that certainly weren't mine. Who else had been here? And had they come in from the apartment where Diantha and I lived?

Alarm swept through me but I chose to remain calm as I looked behind the bar at the stacks of old record books held in the shelves to one side. The old ledgers were covered with dust, and as I pulled one out and opened it up on the bartop, it became apparent after paging through a couple that they were mostly old accounting ledgers for the bar. But one book looked slightly newer. I flipped it open to find the pages were blank, but when I flipped a few more pages, the book kind of fell apart, revealing a square cut out of the interior pages. As I moved to keep the book from slipping out of my grasp, something metal clanged to the floor.

I dropped down to retrieve it, and found a key.

My first thought was the door behind me, but the key didn't fit. Maybe, I thought, it fit on the other side. I pushed the key into my pocket.

"Dahlia?" Amal's voice came from a distance. For whatever reason, I didn't want her to find me here. I closed the book on the bar top and replaced it, and quickly shut off the light and pulled the first door shut, returning the knob to the box and gathering the sheets from the dryer.

"I'm here, Amal," I called back up as I headed for the stairs.

"Owen Sanderson is here," she said.

Time to put one mystery away and focus on the other for a bit. I climbed the stairs, leaving the strange hidden room behind me.

Chapter Sixteen

"Hello, Dahlia," Owen greeted me with a kiss on the cheek and my face immediately flamed with heat.

"Hi Owen," I answered, wishing for once I could control the furious blush and the butterflies that sprang up whenever the detective was around.

Owen wandered over to the side table where there were still a few muffins sitting amid crumbs on the plate.

"Banana?" he asked, peering over his shoulder as he leaned down to sniff.

"Banana oat crumb," I told him.

"May I?" he asked, picking up a plate.

"Of course." It made me happy when he ate the things I'd baked. I knew it was some silly remnant of traditional gender roles and expectations, but I enjoyed the feeling enough not to want to explain it away.

We sat near one another on the couch as Owen tucked into the muffin. I wondered if he ate much when we weren't together. He was always hungry.

"So," I said, hoping I wouldn't have to ask explicitly about the janitor and his confession. I wasn't a police officer, and I knew there was no reason why Owen should share information with me. But I very much wanted him to.

"So," he repeated after swallowing. Then he raised his eyebrows at me and sat back as if he had nothing of particular importance to say.

Meanwhile, I was practically bouncing in my seat, wanting to tell him about the room downstairs, about the principal's odd accounting practices, and Mr. Franklin.

"What shall we talk about?" he asked, picking a crumb off his muffin and popping it into his mouth.

"Well," I said, looking around in frustration but unwilling to push him to tell me about the investigation. "How has your day been?"

"Good," he said lazily. "The weather leaves a bit to be desired. And my shoelace broke this morning on my run. Very inconvenient." He waited for me to speak, but when I added nothing, hoping he'd move on to the topics he knew I wanted to hear about, he went on. "Did you hear they're going to do Peter Pan at the high school this year?"

"No," I said, fighting to keep a conversational tone. "Anything else?"

"Anything specific you were hoping to chat about, Dahlia?" Owen grinned at me as he asked this, and I sensed he was teasing me.

I gave him a wide-eyed look, hoping he wasn't going to make me say it. But of course he was.

Owen chuckled at my discomfort.

"The janitor?" I prodded.

"Angus," he said. Finally we were going to talk about the murder. "Nice fella."

I waited, but Owen busied himself with the muffin wrapper.

"Yes," I said, drawing the word out.

"You can't stand it," Owen laughed.

"What?"

"Not knowing every little thing about the case. Your brain is working forty miles a minute."

I swallowed hard. He wasn't wrong.

"You'd be a good detective, you know."

"So... Angus?"

Owen shook his head. "I don't think he did it."

"He all but admitted it to me," I reminded him.

"It's the 'all but' that matters here. He did get her down to the cove, though."

"Why?" I tried to imagine what Angus could have told Dorothy Withers to make her climb that path when she had a festival to supervise.

Owen sighed and put his plate on the table in front of

us. "He did not intend to kill her," he began. "And I'm fairly certain he didn't do it. He wanted to scare her, I think. He told her there was a group of kids in the cove from the school, vandalizing the rocks with paint."

I shook my head. "I was down there. There was no graffiti."

"There were no kids, either. Angus got her down there and then explained exactly how much he resented the way she had been treating him. He reminded her how fast the tide comes back in and warned her that if she didn't treat him more kindly, he'd bring her down by force and let her drown."

I frowned. I couldn't imagine Angus carrying a struggling Dorothy down the path to the cove, but I guessed that maybe threats didn't have to be super credible to be scary.

"What did she say?"

"Well, she was angry," Owen explained. "She told him that she had little intention of changing her behavior if he didn't change his, and she told him she was going to report him to the principal and the district for threatening her. And then she complained about not being able to climb back up in her heels and skirt, and she berated him for lying to her. She demanded he send someone down to help her up."

"I could understand her anger," I said. "And despite her methods, the fact she went down there really does show that she put the students first. She cared about them."

"Or she enjoyed punishing them."

I thought about that. "She risked her personal safety to try to stop them from doing something they might regret."

Owen gave me a half smile. "That's the optimist's view, at least."

"So how did she end up dead, Owen?"

"I'm not sure, but it wasn't Angus. When he left, she was still down there. The tide was starting to come in, but she wasn't near the rocks."

Someone else must have gone down the path soon after Angus came back up. But who?

"Angus didn't see anyone going down the path as he came up?"

Owen shook his head. "No, and he didn't send anyone down either. He said he saw a few people in the parking lot near the top of the path—Principal Bentley, Mr. Thomas, and Betty Bennett, and he mentioned that she was stuck down there if anyone wanted to help. But he said when he looked back, they were still talking, not heading for the cove."

I wondered on that for a moment—he mentioned she was in trouble, and no one jumped to help. Poor Dorothy.

"Oh, I almost forgot to tell you—Mr. Franklin was very angry at Mrs. Withers that day," I said.

Owen tilted his head. "I did speak to him. He and Sam

167

were in the school most of the morning, working through Sam's latest essay."

"So his son is his alibi?"

"Do you think he'd ask a twelve-year old to lie for him?"

If it kept him out of jail, I thought he might. But I didn't know Mr. Franklin well and it did seem a stretch. "Is there some way to prove they were in the school? Cameras? A time stamp on the computer they were using?"

A smile spread across Owen's face. "I'm telling you, you'd make a great detective, Dahlia. I'll look into that."

I sighed. "I saw Principal Bentley at the festival. With you, remember?"

Owen nodded. "So we know it wasn't him, either. Which leaves us back at square one. I've interviewed Mr. Thomas and Betty, and they both have alibis for the time period when Dorothy was killed. They said they left the parking lot right after Angus came back up and spoke to them, and witnesses confirm that Mr. Thomas arrived on time for his dunk tank turn and Betty Bennett threw the first bean bags to dunk him."

For a moment, we were both quiet, Owen dabbing at the last remaining crumbs of his muffin while I stared into the fireplace, wondering about all the things I'd learned that I hadn't mentioned to Owen yet.

"Have you heard of a group called the Mariners?" I asked him quietly.

Owen stiffened at my side, all attention suddenly shifting from crumbs to my face. "Why? Have you had trouble?"

Eek. Maybe I shouldn't have brought them up until I had something more solid to ask about. "No. What do you mean by trouble?"

"You aren't talking about baseball are you?"

"Afraid not."

He sighed, letting his big body fall back into the cushions of the couch. "Most people don't know about the Mariners. They're not as active here now as they used to be, and some people say they're gone, but they've been around forever. Started as a bootlegging operation during Prohibition and got involved in all kinds of other nefarious dealings after that." Owen squinted at me. "Why are you asking about them?"

I shook my head. "I'm not sure, really. Marcus mentioned them a few days ago, and it's just been stuck in my head." I left out the parts about the lighthouse and the bar downstairs. For now.

"They used to operate around here. They were real, and they were scary. We've done our best to keep them a purely historical group, but they have old connections here, and if I've learned anything in the Department, it's that there are people wrapped up in things you'd never suspect."

That got my attention. "People like the principal? Or maybe Mrs. Withers?"

Owen's face morphed into a frown as he searched my eyes. "You think Mrs. Withers might have been killed by the Mariners? And that Principal Bentley is involved with them?"

"I have no idea. I just wondered."

"Why, Dahlia? You're not making a lot of sense here. A gardener mentioning the group doesn't equate to suspecting they're active again and were involved in a murder."

I let out a long breath. "You're right, it doesn't." I squirmed a little on the couch, attracting Taco's attention, and he moved over to sit on the floor at my feet, staring up at me. "It's okay, boy," I told him. I cleared my throat and told Owen about what I'd learned at the school the other day about the financial records kept for the festival.

"So you think Mrs. Withers was skimming off the top?"

I shook my head. "I don't know. Principal Bentley did not want to discuss it, that was for sure. But I think every point of sale at the festival reports a similar loss every year. He pretty much admitted that."

"That could be a lot of money," Owen said.

I nodded.

"Good lead, Dahlia. There could be something there."

I wasn't going to mention Daisy's snow globe—it still made little sense to me—but I was speaking again before I'd decided to confide in Owen. "There's one other thing," I said.

"Hit me."

"The lighthouse. Salty Shores."

"I'm lost now."

"Daisy had a snow globe. She hid it in the corner of her room in a box full of peanuts. Taco found it."

Owen said nothing, just shook his head softly.

"I know it doesn't really make sense, but I think it's some kind of message. There was a scrap of paper too, with a series of numbers."

"You think she left it for you on purpose? That she knew Taco would find it?"

I shrugged. "I think so. That was how I learned about the Mariners. I guess they have some connection to the lighthouse?"

"They kind of own the place now. It was a whole legal battle about fifty years ago. No one wanted to let a known crime organization own a piece of history, but the historical society didn't have the funds to refurbish the lighthouse and keep it safe for tourists, and they were going to tear it down."

"Why would the Mariners care?"

"Their story is that they're just a group of concerned citizens. A kind of club."

"So they bought the lighthouse?"

"And the land around it," Owen said. "To their credit, the remaining descendants who own the deed now keep the place looking pretty good. You should have seen it before they took over. Leaning to one side, practically crumbling."

"You think they had a reason other than just wanting to preserve it."

"Most people believe that, yeah, but these days, I think it's just an old, inoperative lighthouse."

I thought about that.

"What about the numbers?"

I shook my head. "I haven't figured out what they mean."

"Can I see the note?"

I pulled my phone out of my pocket. I'd tucked the slip of paper into the little wallet that was attached. Removing the paper carefully, I unfolded it and handed it to Owen who frowned down at it, his forehead wrinkling as he considered.

"It's not a phone number. I don't think it's an address."

I didn't think so either.

"Dates? It could be a string of dates."

I hadn't thought of that. I peered down at the line of numbers.

"1/6, 5/3, 6/12, 6/5. If those were dates, would they mean anything to you?"

I shook my head, but my mind went to the ledgers I'd found downstairs. I hadn't dug into them too deeply, but they did contain dates. "I don't know."

Owen looked at the paper a moment longer then handed it back to me, his eyes filled with sympathy. "I think it's possible they don't mean anything, Dahlia. I know you miss your sister..."

"You're right." I stuffed the paper back into my phone case and tucked it away, suddenly eager to end this conversation. I stood.

"Uh..." Owen looked a little startled by my sudden move, but he rose a second later. "I guess I should get back to work."

"Me too."

"I'll see you later?" He looked uncertain, and I couldn't help feeling fidgety and confused. I knew I should tell him the rest, but I didn't want to. I didn't want to hear that there was nothing to figure out, that Daisy was gone and I should let her rest.

I didn't know if I was hanging on to some misplaced idea that she'd left a final message for me, or if there was more to it. Or nothing at all. I did know that it was my mystery to solve, and for now, I wasn't going to involve Owen any more than I already had. Leave the crime to him. This was my sister.

"Sure," I said, stepping around the couch toward the door. "Thanks for telling me about Mrs. Withers."

He nodded and then glanced past me to Amal. "Nice to see you, Amal."

"You too, Detective."

When Owen left, I felt slightly relieved.

Keeping secrets was exhausting.

I didn't sleep well that evening, imagining the sounds of havoc outside in our calm, quiet town. In those dark hours, I was sure it was my unstill mind tormenting me. In the morning, however, I learned it was something else. Something real and terrifying.

Chapter Seventeen

Taco and I stepped out the front door of the inn for our morning walk to find destruction everywhere.

Daisy's garden was in shreds. Plants had been pulled out by the roots, stone paths knocked from the ground, and flowers trampled. Everywhere I looked around the sprawling space, it was exactly the same thing. This wasn't a storm, or a bit of wind damage. This was intentional.

As I surveyed the incredible damage, I let Taco nose around. He seemed every bit as upset as I was, pawing at piles of upended soil and whining.

My heart clenched inside me and my skin felt unnaturally cold. Who would do this? And why? Tears gathered in my throat, burning the backs of my eyes. This was all I'd had left of Daisy. All that lived, anyway.

"Come on, Taco," I managed, surprised how small my voice sounded. "No walk today."

We turned back to the inn's front door and I stopped, my blood icing in my veins. There was a note tacked to the front door, the blocky scrawl legible even from where I stood a few feet away.

"Mind your own business or we come inside next time. - A Friend"

My heart raced as I pulled the note from the door, careful to touch as little of it as possible—could you gather fingerprints from paper? I'd ask Owen.

As I put out breakfast for the morning—just a loaf of quick bread and some sausage and eggs because we had only two full rooms now—I was jittery and upset. And when I stepped back into the lobby, Amal was there, her face white.

"Who did this?" she asked, pointing at the note I'd left on the front desk.

"I don't know," I said, but I wondered if Principal Bentley was capable of something like this. He'd warned me off investigating the school festival's finances any more deeply. But if that was a warning, what was this?

"It's awful," she moaned. "Oh, Daisy..." her eyes filled with tears, and I realized the garden wasn't my connection to Daisy alone. "What will Danny think? This will break her heart."

"I'll drive her to school today and take her out the back to the garage so she won't see," I said. "Maybe Marcus can manage something out there before she gets back."

"Not unless he can work miracles..." Amal said, trailing off sadly.

When Marcus arrived a half hour later, I met him outside.

"Holy moly, you've remodeled," he said, and then blew a low whistle from between his teeth.

"I didn't do this," I told him, though I suspected he was being sarcastic. "It was like this when we got up today."

Marcus's watery eyes were surveying the destruction. "Someone sending you a message?"

I looked at the diminutive man, wondering if I could trust him. Was there any chance he had done this? I pushed the idea away quickly. He'd have no reason to do anything like this. I hadn't wronged him in any way.

"There was a message too," I said, and then I told him what the scrawled note had said.

Marcus's eyes widened. "That's not good. What have you been digging into, Dahlia? Have you been poking around that lighthouse? I warned you not to tangle with those guys."

"I haven't been to the lighthouse," I said. "But I've been looking into a couple other things. But Marcus? It sounds like the Mariners don't operate around here any more." I thought about the footprints in the bar downstairs... could someone have seen mine and realized I was getting close to something?

"They might, they might not. But whatever you're into,

I'd let it go. Dahlia, you're no match for whoever did this. They clearly mean business."

A chill washed through me. I hadn't meant to poke a reviving crime syndicate. I was utterly unprepared for this level of intimidation. But the warning also meant I was on the right path, didn't it?

"Can you do anything out here to put this back together?"

Marcus crossed his arms and looked around. "I'll see what I can salvage. Some of this can be replanted..." he wandered the torn up paths and I followed him. "A lot of it is ruined. I'll have to work a bit longer the next few days." He glanced over his shoulder to see if I flinched, assumedly at the thought of paying him more.

"That's fine," I assured him.

"Better get to work then," he said, and he headed around back to the little garden shed.

I went back inside and announced to Diantha that I'd be taking her to school in the car this morning, telling her I needed to pop in and speak with the principal, something I had no intention of doing. When we arrived at the school, I parked, and made a show of getting out of the car with Taco as Diantha made her way to class. Then we got back in and headed to the police station.

"Good morning," I said to the red-headed policeman at the desk in front. "Is Detective Sanderson in yet?"

"Just arrived," the man said. "I'll let him know he has

company." He rose and returned a moment later, Owen at his side.

"Hey Dahlia. Hey Taco." His smile flickered and his bright eyes narrowed with worry. "What's going on?"

"Do you have a few minutes?" I asked him. Fear and worry spooled together inside me. I needed to let someone know what had happened. Not telling him everything the night before had been a mistake.

"Of course," he said, pulling open the gate that separated the desk from the lobby and ushering me toward a hallway.

As we settled in his office, he gave me another concerned look. "Is everything okay?"

I took a deep breath. "For now, yes, but I need to let you know about a couple things. I may have stumbled into something."

"That sounds bad," he said.

I told Owen about the garden, about the room beneath the inn and how I'd disturbed the dust and left footprints, and about the locked door. I also told him about the key I'd found.

"But I also think it might all have some connection to the festival, and to Principal Bentley."

Owen's eyebrows shot up at that. "The principal?"

"Those books are really bothering me. What administrator would be okay with the idea of his annual event losing that amount of money on a yearly basis?"

He rubbed a hand through his sandy blond hair, sending the waves falling over his forehead. "Yeah, you've got a point."

"I mean... It's irresponsible at best and potentially criminal at worst."

"Right," Owen said, his eyes falling to the blotter on his desk.

"But maybe it's bigger than him," I pointed out. "And maybe he's just a pawn?"

"How so?"

I told Owen about the records I'd found in Mrs. Withers's room. "She was definitely tracking the discrepancies," I said. "I found proof of that. So what if the whole thing is part of the Mariners' organization coming back, and what if she was getting too close to the truth?"

"So they removed her," Owen said, his voice low and wary.

"It makes sense."

Owen blew out a long breath and leaned back in his chair. "I don't like it at all," he said. "They were a dangerous group, and if they're back and involved, then this whole thing is way bigger than you and me. This becomes FBI-level territory."

I nodded, another chill icing my veins.

"Let's go look at the room you found. I don't like the idea that someone can access your apartment. I want to see that note too. I'll bring a fingerprint kit."

"Good. I'm not too worried about anyone accessing the apartment through the room I found," I told him. "They'd have to be inside the hotel to do it." It was the thing I'd been telling myself since discovering the door and the footprints. Only, the footprints had been just inside that locked door—meaning whoever left them had come from inside the door, not the way I'd come from the lobby of the hotel. I suppressed a shiver.

Owen rose, and together we drove Daisy's little car back to the hotel. Entering through the back kept Owen from seeing the destruction out front, and I was glad. I could already sense that he was worried, and even through I'd told him about it, seeing how ripped apart the garden was wouldn't help.

I led him through the hotel's laundry room and to the door, retrieving the doorknob and pulling the door open before switching on the light.

"Rats on a raft," he said, his eyes scanning the space. He was about to step inside when my eyes snagged on something that sent my heart racing. I reached out to grab his sleeve.

"Wait."

"What is it?" His concerned eyes found my face.

"Look at the floor."

Where there had been only my footprints from this door to the other yesterday, now the entire room was disturbed, with footprints everywhere, scattered through the thick dust all around the space.

"Someone else has been in here," I said, my mind racing through the possibilities. Amal? Diantha? One of the guests?

"I don't think there's much evidence to mess up here," Owen pointed out. "These are so scattered and disturbed, it'd be hard to learn much from them. Watch for a single footprint and let's try to preserve any that are intact."

I nodded, following him into the room.

"Can you imagine what this must've been like back when it was operating?" His voice held a tone of admiration, and his eyes scanned the dark maroon walls, lingered on the single chandelier.

"You think it was an actual speakeasy?"

"I'm sure it was," he said. "There are a couple around Saltcliff, mostly in old buildings like this one that have been privately owned for a century."

"There are some old ledgers under the bar," I told him.

Owen moved around, pulling the leather-bound books from their spot. "Mind if I take these for a bit?"

"No," I said. "I do want to look and see if the numbers Daisy left me match any of the dates in those books, though."

Owen sighed lightly and then nodded. "Of course. We can do that upstairs. If these weren't taken, I wonder what the intruders were doing down here. Was there anything else?"

"Nothing obvious." Then again, I'd lived in an inn with a secret room for six months and never knew.

We spent a few more minutes looking around, and then left the room, removing the doorknob once again.

"I'm going to send someone to lock that other door," Owen said. "And give it a good deadbolt with a key only you have."

"That would be a bit of a relief," I agreed.

We returned to the lobby and said hello to Amal who gave us a curious look, then we took the ledgers into the apartment and put them on the dining room table.

"There's one other thing I'd like to see," Owen said. "You said there's a separate basement in here?"

I led him down the rickety stairs to the dark, damp basement beneath the kitchen where we kept luggage and a few boxes of my sister's things. Owen used his phone to illuminate the walls, revealing a door that clearly led in the direction of the speakeasy.

It was locked from this side with a deadbolt, which Owen spun, pulling the door open toward us.

"Does it go into the club?" I asked, peering into the darkness from behind him.

"Maybe," he said, flashing his light into the dark space.

As I stepped in behind him, I didn't see the club as expected. Instead, we were in a tiny hallway, almost a vestibule. Another door stood directly in front of us, and one more lay to the left.

"Another door," I said. "So if that one goes into the speakeasy"—I pointed to the door straight ahead—"where does this one go?"

Owen illuminated the handle of the other door, trying it but finding it locked. "Think your key fits here?"

I dug the key out of my pocket, only a little bit surprised to find it fit into the lock and turned with a smooth click. Owen pulled open the door, and we both sucked in a breath as we took in the view beyond it.

A tunnel. Carved from the earth and supported with beams and metal poles, leading into the darkness.

My mind immediately went to the earthquakes that plagued this region and fear pinged the back of my brain. I couldn't imagine being in here if it collapsed. Then again, it had clearly stood for years.

"Holy mother of cows," Owen said, shaking his head.

"Do we follow it?" I asked.

"Not right now," he said. "But this does explain one thing."

"It does?"

He nodded, pushing the door shut again and relocking it. "The footprints you found inside the speakeasy. They didn't come from your apartment. Someone came inside from this tunnel."

Bumped Off at the Bake Sale

Well. That wasn't especially reassuring. But at least they hadn't been in our home. "But why?"

He shrugged. "Not sure. Let's go back up. This place gives me the willies."

Owen ushered me out of the tunnel and locked the door into the basement, and then we headed back upstairs. My heartbeat regulated as we stepped into the kitchen, which was flooded with sunlight, casting reassurance through my mind.

"Dahlia," Owen said, turning to me with a lopsided grin. "You've just found an even bigger mystery to solve."

Wonderful.

We moved to the dining room table and each of us carefully opened one of the old leather books.

"Wow, look at this," Owen breathed, leaning over the yellowed, lined pages. "This must have been the accounting system the bar downstairs used. These dates are from the twenties."

"And this one looks like inventory," I said, pointing to lines of spirits next to numbers and shipment dates.

"What's in that one, then?"

"This is where the key was," I told him, flipping to the cut out square.

"There's writing there, though," Owen reached for the cover of the book, his fingers brushing mine as he pulled it open more and then flipped back a few pages in the front.

185

"Oh, those are dates. And they look like they've been written more recently."

"Hard to tell," Owen said doubtfully.

But as we peered at the numbers, written in a blocky, unfamiliar hand, they were nearly illegible.

"Do these mean anything to you?" Owen asked.

I pulled Daisy's note out of my phone case and compared. Nothing matched. And Daisy's handwriting was loopy and feminine where this was stark and bold. "Nothing."

For a moment we sat, just looking at the old books, and I wished I could find the connection I wanted. Something to tie the club downstairs to the destruction in my yard, and maybe to the death of Dorothy Withers. But they seemed to hold more historical value than anything else.

"Where do you think that tunnel leads?" I asked Owen.

"I'm going to send a team over to find out," he said. "Please promise me you won't go down there on your own before that."

I shook my head, imagining the dark tunnel. "No worries there."

"Okay with you if I take the note back to the station to run for prints? It'll be easier than trying to do it here."

"Sure," I said, eager to be rid of the ominous warning.

Chapter Eighteen

That evening, Diantha and Amal and I were invited to dinner at Tessa Damlin's house next door.

A locksmith had been by earlier, and the door downstairs was dead bolted, which made me feel much better. Owen had called to tell me that men would be by the next week to explore the tunnels, but he was bringing a full set of safety gear to do it. He also made me promise I wouldn't enter the tunnel first, a promise I had no trouble with.

We gathered up the black forest cake I'd made and Amal carried a bottle of wine, and we headed out the front door of the inn, Taco acting as if the entire event was orchestrated just for him. He practically danced on the end of his leash as we walked out into the cooling air.

As we stepped onto the path, I forgot that Diantha hadn't seen the garden all day, since I'd hurried her in and out the back door before and after school.

"Aunt Dolly..." Amal and I were nearly at the gate when Diantha's voice came through the settling dusk, wavering with uncertainty. "Did you dig up Mom's garden?"

"Oh Danny," Amal said, her voice a near whisper.

"No, I didn't," I said, answering the question but wishing I could think of something more soothing to offer. This was one of those moments when I needed parental instincts I simply didn't have. I took a step closer, sensing that she needed ... something. "It...it was worse when we got up this morning. It was vandalized."

My niece stared at me for a moment, her mouth open in an unspoken question, and then she snapped her mouth shut and gazed around at the still devastated garden. "But... who would do this?"

Did I tell her? I didn't think mentioning that I'd drawn the attention and possibly the ire of a dangerous crime syndicate would help her sleep at night. I didn't want to lie, either.

"I don't really know, Danny." I put a hand on her cheek, careful to balance the cake stand in one hand, and Taco wound his leash around her, pressing himself into her thighs. "Owen is looking into it."

Diantha looked up at me again with tears in her eyes and then stepped into me, wrapping her arms around my waist and burying her face in my sweater. "It was all we had left of her," she said in a broken voice.

I wrapped my arm around her and held her, and it made me feel a little better to be able to offer something, though I was worried about dropping the cake, which was becoming very heavy in my left hand.

"I'm so sorry, Danny. We'll get it put back together."

Diantha sniffed and pulled away, lunging ahead of me on the path and wiping her eyes furiously, as if angry that she'd needed a hug. I followed her out of the garden and to Tessa's door along with Amal.

"There you are!" Tessa cried as we approached her little cottage, which was nearly grown over with ivy. "I worried you'd gotten lost on the way over!"

"We live just next door," I reminded her, and Tessa burst out laughing, her bright lipstick making her mouth seem even larger.

"A joke, Dahlia. We'll have to teach you more about those some time. Come in, ladies! And Taco."

We moved into the small front room of Tessa's cottage, and I was relieved to finally put the cake down on a side table. Taco greeted Albert, Tessa'a elderly grey-hound, and the two of them trotted into the kitchen together.

"Oh, that cake looks lovely," she said, leaning in close to the cake as if to sniff it. Her blocky necklace nearly swiped through the chocolate frosting, but she caught it just in time, holding it to her chest, which was covered in a bright floral muumuu.

"We brought this for you," Amal said, handing her the bottle of wine and giving her a light hug.

Tessa held it up to look at it and clucked appreciatively. "You girls are so good to me. Shall we pop it open, or would you prefer some of the spirits I've got hidden away from the Prohibition era? You know, Grandaddy was a moonshiner."

"Here in Saltcliff?" Amal asked.

"What's moonshine?" Diantha asked.

I'd had some of Tessa's moonshine before. It was strong. To say the least.

"Maybe just some wine," I suggested. "And if you're willing, I'd love to hear about your grandfather." My interest had been piqued. Had he sold spirits to the club under my inn? Or been a regular guest, perhaps?

"He was a common criminal, if you want the truth," Tessa said, busying herself pulling a variety of mismatched wine glasses from the buffet against the wall. "But his nefarious dealings are to thank for all this," she said, waving her arm around to indicate the tiny living room stuffed with tattered furniture and glowing warmly with the light from several lamps.

"Right," I said, accepting a glass and moving to sit on a faded blue armchair in the corner.

Soon, Amal and Tessa sat across from me, and Diantha had taken the dogs out into Tessa's back yard to throw a ball for them.

"I really am interested in hearing about your grandfather," I tried again.

Tessa rolled her eyes. "Ancient history, really. He was part of this group of men who just didn't want to leave well enough alone." She took a healthy sip of her wine and seemed content to say no more.

"What does that mean?" Amal asked, tilting her head.

"Liquor was illegal. Plain and simple. But did my relatives say, 'oh well, better make some more tea then?' No, they did not." Tessa let out a loud cackle that made me jump. "Those yahoos got busy learning to brew all kinds of nearly drinkable liquors in the bathtub and started selling it all over town." She grinned widely, and I sensed she had more pride in her family history than she'd first let on.

"Where did he sell it if it was illegal?" I asked, hoping she would reveal knowledge of the club beneath the inn.

"Here and there," she said. "There was once a speakeasy in the old lighthouse, did you know that?"

"There was?" I asked, sitting up straight.

Tessa nodded, and a timer went off loudly in the kitchen. "Ohh, that'll be the pot pies!" She sprang to her feet and took one more long gulp of wine before depositing her glass on a side table and hustling through the doorway to the back of the cottage.

"Dahlia," Amal said, keeping a careful tone. "Why are you asking so many questions about lighthouses and moonshine?"

191

"Um..." I didn't want to tell Amal I'd endangered us all and was trying to find a way out of it. But she was in danger now too, probably. "I'm trying to understand a bit about the Mariners. They're an org—"

"I know exactly what they are." Amal snapped, her cheeks reddening.

"Oh. Well then. Them."

"That's who ripped apart the garden?"

"Probably. I mean, it seems very likely, yes."

Amal set her glass down and blew out a long breath. "Oh no."

I squinted at her, surprised at her sudden turn of emotion. "Is there something you're not telling me?"

She stared at her wineglass for a long moment and then said, "Actually, there is a lot I haven't told you, and it sounds like I have no choice now. But it needs to wait until we're back at the inn."

I did not enjoy the suspense that statement created.

The suspense lasted throughout the meal, which was excellent, even though Tessa insisted on attempting to tell our fortunes throughout the meal. Ever since she'd held a mock seance for me to convince a widow to tell the truth about her husband's death soon after I'd arrived in town, she was convinced she had actual otherworldly powers.

"I see a handsome man in your future," she told Diantha over her plate of cake and ice cream.

"A man?" Diantha looked mildly disgusted at this idea.

"Yes, a man with dark hair and sunglasses."

"That's kinda weird."

"We see a lot of people walking around town," I pointed out. "I bet Tessa is right. Maybe he'll buy one of your leashes."

"How are sales going, Danny?" Amal asked.

"Tabitha sent me a text yesterday and said she needs at least ten more whenever I can get them done."

"Ten?" I was surprised. "That's great. So she's sold most of what she had, then."

Diantha shrugged. "I guess so."

"How much are they selling for?" Tessa asked, her gaze moving to the corner where Albert and Taco sprawled side by side.

"Twenty-five dollars," Diantha said.

Tessa's eyebrows lifted, and Diantha shrugged. "It's a tourist town. People pay it."

"Smart girl," Tessa said. "But too rich for my blood."

"Tessa," I ventured as the woman pushed back her plate.

Her eyebrows rose in question.

"I wondered if you might be able to help us with something at the inn." Heat rose in my cheeks because I knew both Diantha and Amal would think this was a bit silly, but after all that had happened, I felt like I needed to take some kind of action. "Would it be possible for you to try to get rid of our ghost? He's frightening the guests and... dogs."

"Dogs?"

"One dog."

"Well, either way, sure. I can come sage and do some clearing work."

I wasn't eager for her to come tonight, because I knew Amal wanted to tell me something important. "Tomorrow?"

"You got it," Tessa said, winking.

The evening wound down soon after that, and I found myself rushing through the cold air outside to get back to the inn so Amal could share whatever secret she'd been keeping.

We headed inside and got Taco and Diantha situated for bed, and then Amal gestured for me to go back out into the lobby with her. It was late, and there were no guests around, so we sat on the long couch before the fire, which was glowing embers.

"Dahlia, I think you should stop digging into whatever it is you think you've found."

"What I've found is an abandoned club beneath the inn, accessible via a tunnel that leads off into the darkness." I watched Amal's expression as I told her about the club, the tunnel, the door from our basement, and her eyebrows climbed slowly. "It's the reason I was so curious about Tessa's story. I think it's all linked. And if there is a crime syndicate operating, it's totally possible that Principal Bentley is involved, maybe involuntarily. It could be extortion," I explained. "And they might have killed Dorothy Withers."

Amal's face blanched and she reached into her red leather bag and pulled out a small book, handing it to me slowly, as if it pained her to let it go. "This is your sister's."

"What is it?" I took the small leather-bound notebook and turned it over in my hands. It was about the size of a notecard, and a string wrapped around it, holding it shut.

"When Daisy... died," Amal said, struggling with the word. "She was in the midst of something."

She was in the midst of life, I figured. What else? "Go on."

"She'd been published a few times—I don't know if you knew that."

I shook my head. Published? "What did she write?"

"Investigative journalism. She had a couple pieces about coastal pollution and one on a farm that was supposedly using eco-friendly practices but actually used all the same pesticides everyone else does. They were charging more for their products."

"I didn't know Daisy was doing that," I said.

Amal tilted her chin down, her gaze trained on her hands in her lap. "She was passionate about it, about justice, about things being done the right way."

"She was like that when we were children too. She

liked making sure everything was fair." Which suited me fine because when we had to split something in half, I enjoyed the process of measuring and dividing evenly. Daisy enjoyed knowing everyone got the same amount.

"It became almost an obsession as she pursued the last thing she was working on."

"What was that?"

Amal lifted her dark gaze. "She never told me explicitly. But it was something serious. Something potentially dangerous."

"Oh." I wasn't sure what to say, but suspected Amal knew something more. She'd linked whatever she needed to say to the Mariners earlier, hadn't she?

"When she... once she was gone," she went on. "I did some digging. I found some notes she'd left on my computer one night when she was working at my place."

"Notes about what?"

"About the Mariners, I suspect. I think Daisy was tracking their operations. I think she was planning to expose them."

I flipped open the little leather book. Each page was labeled with a date at the top, and next to the date was a name.

Mayor Spindell. Principal Bentley. Councilman Yarrow. Beneath the names were notes. But the notes made little sense. They said things like, Hilldale storefront, September 21 and Gonser Building, June 14. All of the people on the notes were powerful in their realms. Mayor Spindell was the mayor of the next town over, if I remembered correctly.

"So these people in the book? But what do these notes mean?"

Amal shrugged, her face full of worry. "Maybe she thought they were covering something up. Like maybe they were members? Maybe the locations were meetings?"

"I've been wondering about that. About the principal, at least. Or maybe he's a pawn for a much bigger nefarious operation." It sounded ludicrous, but anything was possible. "And... what happened?"

"That's when Daisy got sick. Very sick. It was aggressive, and it took her so fast. But I think she was worried she'd uncovered something dangerous—something that might put us at risk."

"Amal, do you really think the Mariners are still active?"

Amal hesitated, then shook her head. "I don't know. Daisy was convinced she was onto something big. Something that could make powerful people very angry if she exposed it. But she never told me exactly what it was. It might have had to do with them, and then maybe not."

I flipped through more pages in the book. At the top of one page, the name Amanda Steele was listed. For some reason, the name was familiar to me.

"Amanda Steele? Why do I know this name?"

"She was a prominent journalist in San Francisco. Daisy reached out to her for advice on how to handle her findings. They met a few times, but Amanda went missing shortly afterward. Daisy feared the same thing might happen to her if she didn't tread carefully."

I felt a chill run through me. Was my digging just opening the same doors Daisy had been afraid of? But she'd left me hints, as if she'd wanted me to pursue this. "I'm not sure what to do."

Amal's eyes filled with tears, and she nodded slowly. "Keep your eyes open. Daisy wasn't sure what was going on, but she was pretty sure not everyone around here was playing by the rules."

I nodded, the weight of this new responsibility settling on my shoulders. Suddenly, I wasn't just trying to figure out who killed Dorothy Withers. I was also trying to finish whatever my sister had begun. I wasn't sure why it felt important to do it, but it did. For Daisy.

Chapter Nineteen

Tessa Damlin was at the door early the following morning, holding a basket and wearing a variety of colorful silken scarves.

"Ready to banish your ghostly presence," she announced.

I waved her in and showed her to the Holden suite. "Should I stay?" I asked as I watched her remove a variety of items from her basket and begin placing them around the room.

"Better if you don't," she said, glancing at me as if just realizing I was still there. "You can be distracting."

"Oh."

I left her to her work and went back downstairs. An hour later, she reappeared in the lobby.

"All set," she said. "I'll waive my usual fee, since we're girlfriends."

Before I could answer, she'd trundled back out the front door.

Well. I hoped that might actually work, but my hopes were not especially high.

Diantha and I took Taco into town the following day for the weekly farmer's market, which was close to shutting down for the winter season. It was a kind of meet and greet, the sort of thing I would have avoided in my previous life, but which I enjoyed now—in small doses, at least.

The market was on Nutmeg Street for just a few hours in the afternoon, and during that time the street was closed to traffic. The scenery had changed since the summer, and now in place of bright sunflowers and tables of ripe red tomatoes, there were vendors selling huge pots of mums and all kinds of seasonal squash.

Taco loved the energy and the presence of so many of the town's canine residents, and Diantha enjoyed the chance to choose a few things to go into the next week's breakfast offerings at the inn. The wheeled cart we strolled with was full of butternut squash, beets, and persimmons, and I was already envisioning adding beets to some dense fudge brownies and trying my hand at a traditional pudding made with persimmons.

"Aunt Dolly, there's Principal Bentley."

The principal was bent over, examining a jar of local honey at the stall next to us, and while I wasn't especially eager to engage, given our last interaction, Diantha had already called hello in his direction.

We stepped near and I did my best to look friendly. Taco had no such concerns, shoving his head immediately into the principal's hand for a pet.

"Errr. Hello," the principal said, looking less than happy to see us. He had dark purple marks around his eyes today, and a white bandage across the bridge of his nose.

"Did you hurt yourself, Principal Bentley?"

The man straightened and cleared his throat. "Yes, yes. Not a big deal. Just some boxing classes I take. And, you?" He said, looking at Diantha with a fatherly expression. "How is school going?"

"Pretty good, I think," my niece answered, not making eye contact.

I, too, was looking at the ground as he spoke, working on forcing myself to meet his eye. Sometimes it was hard. But as I examined the principal's shoes, I noticed a thin white line along each leather loafer, just above the sole. The leather beneath the line was slightly darker than that above it. The same thing had happened to a pair of my shoes—the pair I'd worn in the cove when I'd gone down to see the scene of Dorothy Withers's death.

"And Dahlia? How's business?" There was an odd tone in the principal's voice, and now I did look up to see if I could read anything by his expression, but his face appeared open and calm as ever.

"Good," I said. "The inn has been filling up ahead of the holidays."

"Well, that's good to hear," he said. "I love when local businesses are succeeding. Especially those occupying such valuable old buildings." He tucked his chin to look at Taco, giving him a quick pat. "If things ever go south, you know... you'd have no trouble finding buyers."

"Ah, well. Okay." I pondered that as the principal waved and moved on toward a booth selling alpaca yarn and needlework supplies.

"Ohh, Aunt Dolly, should we get some yarn too? You can finally show me how to make the dog sweaters?"

I did owe Diantha some lessons. We'd gotten distracted by the investigations I seemed to keep getting pulled into.

"Good idea."

We visited several more booths, finishing our shopping at Valerie's booth with a couple hot ciders and iced pumpkin cookies before heading back to the inn. Sundays were my favorite days there. They began with a big break-fast spread, and then Diantha and I usually spent the after-noons together.

"Hey," I said, an idea springing into my brain. "Want to finish up our day with a quick trip to the lighthouse? I've never seen it."

Diantha gave me a funny look, and shook her head, sending her now-shoulder length hair dancing around her shoulders. "You're obsessed with this lighthouse."

"You want to go or not?"

She put a finger to her bottom lip and looked down at Taco, who was practically sitting on my feet. "What do you think, Taco? Lighthouse?"

Taco was game for anything, any time. He got to his feet and his tongue lolled out of one side of his mouth.

"That's a definitive yes," I told her.

"Then I guess we're going to the lighthouse."

A half hour later, we got out of the car in front of the Salty Shores lighthouse, which sat on a prominent spit of land north of Saltcliff. From here I could see the coves beneath our town, along with the sandy beach that spanned the length of the biggest cove, where people walked and jogged with dogs at their sides. To the north were more rocky outcroppings, certainly not a friendly place for boats, especially considering the typical fog we got here so often.

"We can't go inside," Diantha reminded me in a tone that said she was merely tolerating my desire to see the old historical building, as one might allow a child a quick trip to the zoo.

"I know," I said. But I wondered. I strode to the red door at the back, my hand reaching for the key I'd been carrying around since I found it. It wasn't very likely, but I thought I'd give it a try anyway.

"Where'd you get that?" Diantha asked when I pulled the key out and tried it in the lock.

As the key turned and the door unlatched, my niece stared at me. "What's going on?"

"Just lucky, Danny. I found this key, and I thought it might work here."

"That's super weird," she said as I pulled the door open.

"Hey!" A voice came from the dusky interior, followed quickly by another.

"Dude! Run!"

The sounds of scrambling feet filled the air, and another door clanged across the dim space. Dust floated in the wake of whoever had just departed as I stepped inside.

"Someone was in here?" Diantha asked, looking worried.

"I guess so," I said. "They sounded young."

"Yeah, like my age maybe," Diantha said.

We peered around the open space. The dusty floor was made up of wide wooden planks, and grey light came in from slit windows high overhead.

"Aunt Dolly, look." Diantha stood in the middle of the space, pointing at something lying on the floor.

"What is that?" I asked, stepping closer.

"It's one of those twenty-sided dice."

It was. And it was sparkly red, imprinted with gold numbers. "What in the world?"

"The kids at school use these to play D and D." Diantha leaned over and picked it up before I could suggest it might need to be fingerprinted. But then I realized what was going on here.

"So it was kids in here," I said. "And they were probably just playing Dungeons and Dragons."

"Weird," Diantha said again, pocketing the die. She cast a guilty look at me. "I can keep it, right?"

"Sure, I don't see why not. I don't think they're coming right back for it."

She chewed her bottom lip. "They might come back though, I guess." I watched, a flicker of pride glowing in me as my niece took the die back out of her pocket and set it on the sill of the single window that was reachable from this floor.

Taco pulled me across the space, nosing at a trap door cut into the floor on the far side. I knelt next to it, and then pulled the rope handle to open it.

"What's that?" Diantha was at my side in a rush. "Wow, a tunnel? Is that where they went?"

I hadn't told her about the tunnel beneath the inn, but the two were most likely connected. Possibly in a literal sense. I needed to tell Owen.

"Yep, I think so. There are no other doors in here." I let the door shut quietly and got to my feet.

We investigated a bit more inside the lighthouse, even climbing the steel stairs that rose up to the top of the tower. As long as we were inside, I figured, we might as well get the full tour, and the steps looked sturdy enough. The views from the top were stunning—the deep midnight blue of the Pacific stretched to the horizon, the sun lighting the surface in glittering sparkles as it moved closer to the line that would separate day from night. The sky was streaked with red and orange near the horizon, and a darkening blue above. It was breathtaking.

When we finished up, I locked the door again and pocketed the key.

"I still think it's weird that you have a key," Diantha said.

"Yeah." It was weird. But I didn't want to tell her where I'd gotten it yet. "You ready to get back and do some baking?"

She nodded. "I really don't know what you're going to make with beets though. Yuck."

"Wait until you see how they make chocolate taste," I promised.

"No thanks."

We climbed back into the Fiat, Taco happily piling himself into the tiny back seat, and headed home.

I was just getting ready to turn in for the night when my phone lit up on the nightstand. Owen.

"Hi," I said.

"Hey you."

"How was your weekend?" I knew he'd been busy coordinating with federal agencies to alert them to the potential that the Mariners were operating again here, and he was probably lining up the team to explore the tunnels we'd found.

"Busy. But I've got a few guys coming in tomorrow to dig into this Mariners thing. Dahlia, if these guys are operating here again, this could be big."

"Yeah, I guess so," I agreed. "I found something else, Owen."

I could almost hear his frown. "I don't like you digging around in this one, Dahlia. If those guys are involved, this goes way deeper than just the death of a schoolteacher."

"Well, I still need to tell you what I learned today."

"Okay, go ahead."

"There are kids in those tunnels."

"What? Dahlia, I warned you not to go in there."

"I didn't. I went in the lighthouse."

"Do I even want to know how you got into a locked historical site?"

"I have no way of knowing what you want to know," I told him. "But I'll tell you anyway. I used the key. It worked on the lighthouse door, and there's a trap door in there that leads to a tunnel just like the one downstairs."

"I knew about that trap door. It's part of why the lighthouse is kept locked."

"Well, someone else has a key," I said. "Or knows where another entrance to the tunnels is. When we unlocked the door, there were kids in there."

"Kids?" Owen's voice rose. "Doing what?"

"I think they were playing Dungeons and Dragons, but they ran when they heard us coming in."

"Ran?"

"Into the tunnel."

"Oh man, that's not good. All we need is a bunch of kids running into the guys in that crime syndicate. This just keeps getting worse."

I changed the subject. "Hey, did you find any record of Mr. Franklin and Sam in the school building at the time of death?"

"Yeah, actually. They logged into the computer lab about twenty minutes before Mrs. Withers went to the cove, and they were in there for about two hours."

"And Angus has an alibi?"

"He's still trying hard to confess, but there are several witnesses to him sampling cookies at three booths on the far side of the field at the same time that Mrs. Withers would have been down in the cove. He may have led her there, but he didn't actually stay down there with her. So even if his actions led to her death, someone else went down there to finish the job."

"I see." I still didn't know who could have been in the cove with Mrs. Withers, but I had a thought. "I saw the principal today," I remembered. "At the farmer's market."

"Yeah?"

"His shoes had salt stains on them. And his nose was broken."

"Dahlia, this is called a non-sequitur."

"No, it's related."

"How?"

"My shoes also have salt stains." I thought about the shoes I'd feared were ruined after visiting the cove. Of course, in my case, they were actually Daisy's shoes.

"You've lost me," Owen sounded amused.

"I think the principal was in the cove. That's how his shoes got stained."

"Ahh, yeah. That makes sense. But it's not really solid evidence. Anyone who lives near the ocean probably has a pair of shoes with salt stains, don't you think?"

"I guess so, yeah." It was my first pair of salt-stained shoes, but Owen was right. The water could have gotten to them on any beach. It wasn't evidence at all.

"Plus," Owen reminded me. "We saw the principal at the bake sale."

"Right." We had. We definitely had.

"How'd his nose get broken? Owen asked.

"He said boxing classes."

"Doesn't seem like his kind of thing," Owen said.

A brief silence filled the line. Then I asked, "So who's the most likely suspect at this point?"

"I think we just tipped over the point of appropriate sharing for info on an active investigation. I've told you too much already, and I need to do a better job of maintaining a clear line between work and us."

Of course he did. I'd been pushing, and I knew it was unfair to expect Owen to share details with me. "Probably for the best."

"I'm sorry," Owen did sound sorry. Or sad. "The lines are blurring, you know?"

I did not. It was this kind of figurative language that always confused me. "Lines?"

"Between us. Talking as colleagues, and talking as friends, and maybe talking as something more?" He sounded unsure as he ended this explanation, making it a question.

"Because of the date?"

"Yes. Because of that."

"I'm sorry if I'm making it hard to do your job, Owen." I wasn't sure what to say. My heart was beating a little faster than I was used to, as if something important hinged on this conversation.

"You aren't. The real problem is that the closer I get to you, the more I'd like to just tell you everything."

Oh. Well. "That is a kind thing to say."

"It's not. It's a selfish thing to say. It's something you

say to someone you think you're dating but who doesn't seem to be one hundred percent sure she wants to be dating you."

Were we dating? Did I want to be dating? I had so little experience in this realm, I didn't know how to answer at all. "Oh." That probably wouldn't suffice.

Owen sighed.

Yep, that had not been sufficient. "Owen, I..."

"It's pretty late, Dahlia."

I looked at the time on my phone. It was late. And I hadn't gotten ahead on the baking for the week because of the last-minute trip to the lighthouse. "Okay."

"I'll catch up with you soon, okay?"

"Good night."

"Good night."

I put my phone on the bedside table, an uncomfortable feeling lingering somewhere between my stomach and my heart. I'd said something wrong, but I wasn't sure what the right thing would have been.

Chapter Twenty

Monday I was up early to bake muffins and a quiche for the morning's breakfast spread. I looked longingly at the beets and persimmons I'd picked up at the market, but forced myself to concentrate. Those recipes would have to wait, especially since I'd need to test a little bit with both, because I'd never made either one before.

Baking was the only thing I seemed to have an instinct for.

Very unlike my interpersonal relationships—especially the one that seemed to have been developing with Owen—baking just made sense to me. I knew that the addition of beets to chocolate would enhance not only the sweetness, but also the moistness of the cake and add a kind of intangible element people would enjoy.

Why couldn't I figure out what made human relationships work well just as easily?

My stomach felt a little upset as I put out the breakfast spread and saw Diantha off to school.

"You okay?" Amal asked after a quick scan of my face.

"I'm fine," I said. Then I updated her on the conversation I'd had with Owen, including the discovery of the kids using the tunnels at the lighthouse.

"I don't think there's a lot to worry about," she said. "From what I know of Owen, he's a pretty straightforward guy. He doesn't play games, and he doesn't lead anyone on, I don't think."

"That's good, at least." I wondered if it was possible that with my complete lack of relationship know-how, I needed something even more basic than straightforward guys. Or maybe I just wasn't made to have a partner at all. The thought made me sad, but I swallowed it down. Right now, I didn't need a partner. I needed to get into the little Fiat and head up to San Francisco. I had a plan.

"You can go. I'll be okay here today," Amal said after I'd explained what I needed to do. "But Dahlia, be careful."

I got Taco's travel bag and leash, and together we headed out to the garage. Soon, I was on my way north to the last place of employment of writer Amanda Steele.

As I drove, my head spun with the possibilities of what might have happened to her. I'd done a little Googling after seeing her name in Daisy's journal, and she'd written exposes on big businesses on the west coast—highlighting fraudulent practices and outing executives who were playing by their own rules. And then she'd gone missing.

Taco and I found a place to park with relative ease, and stepped out onto the smooth wide sidewalks in front of the building where Amanda had worked. The Examiner was housed in a tall steel and glass monolith with a stern-looking man guarding the desk in the lobby.

"Appointment?" he asked, eyeing Taco with suspicion.

"Um, no," I admitted. "I was just hoping I might be able to speak to someone about a writer who used to work at the Examiner."

The man raised a dark eyebrow at me and then tilted his head to the side. "Service animal?"

"Yes, sir. This is Taco. He is an allergen dog."

"Sign in here."

I did as directed, and waited while he snapped a picture and gave me a badge with the photo on it and my name, and then directed me to the tenth floor.

At the desk in the lobby on floor ten, a young woman smiled when she saw Taco and came around the desk, ignoring a ringing phone.

"Ohhh, hello," she said, only glancing up at me for a second as she knelt in front of Taco Dog. "May I?" She held a hand out to him.

"Sure," I said. Taco was frequently more popular than

I was. I was used to it. He also tended to soften the hearts of those who had reason to turn me away.

"What are you guys here for? Can I help you?" She continued focusing on Taco as she asked this.

"I was hoping you might be able to tell me a little bit about one of your writers. Amanda Steele?"

"Amanda?" The girl looked up at me with a grin. "Yeah, she just got back, actually. Want me to see if she has a minute?"

"Back?"

"From the longest freelance assignment ever. It was nuts - she couldn't tell anyone where she was. Some bajil-lionaire wanted her to travel around with him and do this whole expose thing to prove he wasn't actually the crazy guy all the social media junkies think he is. I think it comes out next week."

So she hadn't disappeared. Not really. That was a relief. "I see."

The woman finally got up off the floor and seemed to realize there were now three different rings coming from the phone at her reception desk. "Dang it," she said. "Give me just a minute and I'll give her a call," she said. Then she pulled on a headset and said, "Examiner, can you hold?"

I sat with Taco for a few minutes while she handled the backlog of calls and while she called back to Amanda. Fifteen minutes later, a tall woman with a shock of red hair appeared at the glass doors. "I'm Amanda," she said, looking around the lobby before her gaze landed on me. "Can I help you?"

I stood. "I hope so. I'm Dahlia. I think you knew my sister? Daisy Vale?"

Amanda's shoulders slumped slightly. "Yes. I was so sorry to hear of her death. I'm so sorry," she said. "Please, come on back. Daisy was a great person. A great journalist too."

One more thing I'd never gotten the chance to know about my sister. I swallowed down the lump of sadness in my throat and took a seat in the little conference room Amanda led me to.

"So what's up?" she asked. "Can I get you coffee or anything?"

"No thanks." I told Amanda about the journal Amal had given me and my suspicions that Daisy had gotten in too deep in some investigation involving the Mariners.

"The bootlegger guys from the twenties?" Amanda asked, cocking her head.

"I think they're active again. Maybe into some kind of extortion?"

Amanda scratched her cheek and then frowned. "Huh. If they are, I haven't heard anything about it. At any rate, Daisy wasn't looking into the Mariners, as far as I know. She was digging into some kind of fraud involving historical buildings in that cute little village where she had the inn."

"I'm running the inn now," I told Amanda. "In Saltcliff."

"Right, yeah. There was some kind of real estate grab going on—or that's what she thought. Something about the town devaluing historic properties on paper so bigwigs could snatch them up for cheap. Then I guess, they'd renovate and put them on the market for their real value, touting the historical status and make a killing."

"That's pretty shady," I said, thinking of the names in the journal Amal had given me. "You were helping her with this?"

Amanda nodded. "She had me dig up a few of the records of recent sales. An old strip of storefronts on Ginger, and the former fire station."

"Anything interesting?"

"Oh yes, very interesting. Like I said, both were historical, but had recent valuations by the city that were way under market. One was bought by a mayor from a nearby town, I think, and one by a school administrator."

"A principal, maybe?"

"I think so," Amanda said. "It sounded like it had been going on for at least a decade, and Daisy was close to exposing the whole thing when she got sick."

I sighed. So many things unfinished. I squeezed my eyes shut for a moment, suddenly overcome with a fierce longing for my sister. For the sister I'd known ten years ago, at least.

Chapter Twenty-One

I drove home, my mind spinning as I tried to piece together everything I'd learned. There were still so many questions.

Were the Mariners active again? If they were, it would explain the threat, the destruction of the garden, and the footprints in the speakeasy beneath the inn. But I was starting to think there could be another explanation for those things. I just didn't know quite what it was.

And if Amanda was right, and Daisy hadn't been on the trail of the Mariners, but someone much more contemporary, could one of those powerful real estate purchasers be the culprit in destroying our garden?

And then the big question lingered. How in the world did Dorothy Withers figure into all of it? Or was it just a horrible coincidence of timing?

I parked the car and went inside, happy to see that

Marcus had made some progress putting the garden back together. Where there had been destruction just a couple days earlier, now the paths were tidy once again and many of the plants had been trimmed back, but were looking healthy and green. I missed all the lovely flowers that had been destroyed, but knew Marcus would do his best to get them growing again as soon as possible.

Inside, several guests were sitting around the lobby, reading or talking quietly in front of the fire. I caught Amal's eye and she raised an eyebrow in question.

"I learned a lot," I told her, moving to stand at her side after greeting a couple guests. Taco headed straight for his water bowl and then flopped onto his bed, exhausted from our outing. "First of all, Samantha Steele is healthy and well and back at work."

"Oh, well that's good," Amal said.

I explained the rest of what Amanda had told me, and Amal nodded. "That makes sense, given what little Daisy said to me about the research. She didn't want to tell me too much, to implicate me, I guess."

"Owen was here almost all day," Amal said. "I hope it's okay that I let them into the basement through the apartment."

"That's fine," I said. "Did he bring the team to search the tunnel?"

She nodded. "There's a network of tunnels under half the town."

"Really? More than just the one here?"

"Some are crumbling and dangerous, but they think they were used by bootleggers back in the days of Prohibition. There are secret doors in several old buildings, some private residences."

That made sense, since we had one here and I'd seen the one at the light house.

"They blocked the tunnels off and shored some of them up with reinforcements. I think they are planning to fill some of them in."

"It's a wonder they've never collapsed," I said, thinking of the earthquakes that were so common in Northern California.

"The scariest thing is that he said there was a lot of evidence of kids using the tunnels. What if something had happened while they were in there?"

I thanked my sister silently for raising her daughter to be smart enough not to climb around in abandoned underground tunnels. "I'm glad they closed them off."

"Dahlia?" Amal said, looking at me thoughtfully.

"Yes?"

"I'd like to see the club you mentioned. The one under the inn."

"Sure. Have a minute?"

Amal nodded and I took her down to the laundry, retrieving the door handle to the hidden room.

When I pulled the door open, she gasped. "I would

never have noticed this. How did you even know to look for it?"

"I didn't really, but I noticed the hole where the handle went."

"I'd never even seen that, it's so dark down here in the laundry. Do you think Daisy knew?"

"I think she did," I said. I told Amal about the hidden key and about the lighthouse snow globe my sister had hidden for me.

Amal stared at me a long moment. "But there's really nothing to prove that Daisy was ever down here," she pointed out. "I don't think she knew about it. I'm certain she would have said something."

I thought back over what I'd seen and found in the little bar room. Amal was right—there was nothing here to prove that my sister had ever been here. I'd assumed that Daisy had hidden the key for me to find in the book. But what if the key had been hidden long before Daisy owned the inn? What if it had been only my longing for my sister that had led me to believe everything I was finding was somehow linked to her?

"I think you're right," I said.

"You know what would be kind of fun?" Amal asked, smiling at me with a light dancing in her eyes.

Fun wasn't something I'd been thinking about lately, and the word sounded almost foreign. "What?"

"If we cleaned this out and got it operating again. Speakeasies are very fashionable now."

"We don't have a liquor license, do we?"

Amal laughed with glee. "I mean, I bet the original bar didn't either." But she took a breath and added. "If we did it though, it would need to be on the up and up."

"It's an idea," I agreed. Did I want people who were not guests at the inn dropping in to drink at our laundry room bar? I'd need to mull the idea over. "Let's think about how it would work."

"Deal," she said.

Together, we headed back upstairs, hiding the door handle in the box where I'd found it.

When Danny came home from school, the three of us went into the apartment to have dinner together. Amal made a steaming chicken soup with rice and I made biscuits. "This is my favorite time of year," Diantha said, leaning close to blow on her spoon as she dipped it into her soup.

"Why's that?" Amal asked her. "Costumes? Trick or treating?"

Diantha shook her head. "That's fun too, though. Aunt

Dolly?" She tilted her head to look at me. "Can we dress Taco up for trick or treating this year?"

I looked over at Taco who was curled into a circle on his kitchen mat. He would have preferred to lie under Diantha's seat in case she dropped crumbs, which she reliably did, but we'd compromised on a designated spot for him to occupy in the kitchen instead.

"What would we dress him as?" I asked her.

Diantha turned and looked at Taco, who raised his head to look back at us, clearly understanding that he was the topic of conversation.

"A unicorn?"

"A dark brown unicorn?" Amal asked, laughing.

"Have you ever seen a unicorn?" Diantha asked her.

"Well, no."

"Right, so you don't know that they aren't brown." I smiled at my niece's use of logic to explain her position, a little glow of pride lighting inside me.

"Fair," Amal said, chuckling as she bit into a biscuit.

"Maybe a hot dog. I've seen some funny hot dog costumes," Diantha went on.

"We'll talk more about it," I promised. "He's never been dressed up before. He might not like it."

"Or he might love it," Diantha said, grinning.

My phone rang as we cleared the table, and I left Diantha and Amal to clear the dishes and stepped out into the living room. "Hi Owen." I still felt a little awkward about how our last conversation had ended. The balance between us was off, I knew. He'd told me he wanted to be dating, and I hadn't reassured him as he might have hoped.

"Hey Dahlia, how are you?"

"I'm good," I told him.

"Good," he said. "I got some prints off the note the vandals left for you, but we don't have a match for them."

"Okay," I said, a little disappointed. I had an urge to keep Owen on the phone, so I searched for another topic. "Amal says you got the tunnels all locked up."

"For now, yes. We're going to go in and reinforce a few and shut some others down totally. There's no need for them now, but one might be useful at some point because it offers another route into a pretty inaccessible part of the peninsula."

"That makes sense."

"Danny doesn't run around down there, does she?"

"I don't think so. No."

"Some kids from the school have been in those tunnels," he went on. "They were bold enough to scratch their names into the walls."

"That wasn't especially wise."

"Kids in middle school aren't generally looked to for wisdom," he laughed.

"True."

"One of the tunnels actually led to a spot on the cliff wall over the cove where Dorothy Withers died."

Surprise wound through me. "Do you think whoever killed her might have escaped that way?"

"Unless he or she could climb a sheer cliff wall, I'd say no. The entrance is about forty feet over the beach."

"Oh, I see," I said, imagining an opening over that cove high up in the cliff wall.

"Except for the defensive bruising and the broken hand, Angus is actually looking like the most likely culprit. He made us come search his house, and he has tide maps all over the walls. He's a guy who knew exactly when the tide was going to be rising in that cove, that's for sure." I wondered what had made Owen feel like it was okay to confide in me about this now, when he'd stopped himself earlier.

"Should you be telling me this?"

"I'm stuck, Dahlia. I need your brain."

I thought about what he'd said about the tide. "Well, the water didn't kill Dorothy Withers."

"And as much as I keep telling myself she got all those bruises and broken bones scrambling onto the rocks, I just don't think it's true."

"How did she break her hand, do you think?"

Owen took a moment to answer. "It would make sense if she was trying to fight someone off. But she would have had to have hit the person pretty hard."

"Mrs. Withers was pretty feisty in general. I could imagine her punching someone."

He blew out a long breath on the other end of the line. "I suppose."

I thought about the principal's nose, but that had happened after Dorothy Withers had been discovered. I'd seen him before the farmer's market and he was fine—or maybe not totally fine... "You know what?" I said, remembering Principal Bentley and his strange way of talking when I'd met him at his office right after the murder. "Could she break her hand hitting someone in the jaw?"

"I suppose, if she hit hard enough. Might break a jaw if it was hard enough to break her hand."

"Principal Bentley was talking funny right after the murder."

"Dahlia, we know it wasn't him. We saw him ourselves at the festival right after it happened. And I'm not sure funny talking counts as evidence."

We had seen him. And we'd spoken to him.

"So where does that leave us?"

"Without a suspect."

I actually had a pretty good idea who the suspect was, but until I had all the pieces, I wasn't ready to accuse him. "Owen?"

"Yeah?"

"I'll talk to you tomorrow, okay?"

"Sure. Good night Dahlia."

"Good night."

I hung up the phone and flipped open my laptop, sending a quick email with a request to Amanda Steele.

Chapter Twenty-Two

I had no response from Amanda when I awoke the next morning, and as much as I wanted to dive into the depths of whatever my sister had been figuring out when she died, I had baking to do.

Amal manned the inn while I spent the better part of the day in the kitchen, testing exactly how much pureed beet would make the chocolate texture I was imagining. It turned out to be more than I thought, but not an extreme amount. (The amount I'd expected and the excessive amount had resulted in dry and sloppy brownies, respectively.)

Once I'd mastered the brownies, I set them aside, turning to the pudding. Though I'd grown up believing pudding was a creamy substance usually served in a bowl (preferably topped with Cool Whip), traditional puddings were much closer to a dense cake, and the one I had in mind would have probably been steamed if made in England, but I was planning to bake it.

I spent some time carefully pureeing the persimmons after peeling them, enjoying the unusual scent and feel of the fruit, which I hadn't gotten to work with in a very long time. When I'd finished mixing and the pudding was in the oven, the scent was almost indescribable.

"It smells like fall in here!" Diantha called, dropping her book bag to the floor and stepping into the kitchen to do a quick turn in the middle of the floor with her nose turned up and her arms out, sending her plaid skirt flying around her legs.

"Like fall?" I asked, smiling at her.

"Yes," she said, stumbling slightly as she stopped spinning. "Like scarves and sweaters, and tea, and cookies and crunchy leaves!"

"It does smell good," said an unfamiliar voice. The voice was followed by a boy who stepped into the kitchen behind Diantha. "Hello Mrs. Vale," he said. "I'm Caleb."

The boy from the bake sale. The one Diantha had said was 'weird.'

"Hi Caleb. You can call me Dahlia. And that," I said, indicating the dog who had leapt to his feet and was nosing eagerly at Caleb, "is Taco. Are you okay with big dogs?"

Caleb grinned and dropped to his knees, letting Taco sniff and lick his face. "I love them," the boy said.

I tried to evaluate my niece without being too obvious.

I'd been given no indication that we would be having company today. Was this a friendship? Something more? "What are you up to today, kids?"

"We have a project," Diantha said, her voice taking on an irritated tone. "Ecosystems or something. We have to make a box."

"A diorama," Caleb explained. "Of a Pacific kelp bed and its ecosystem."

"Ooh, interesting," I said.

"Can we have brownies first?" Diantha asked, eyeing the cooling brownies on the counter.

"I think that would be okay. Caleb, would your parents mind if you had a brownie?"

The boy shook his head, sending his lanky hair over his eyes. He was skinny, and I figured a brownie couldn't possibly hurt him.

"No allergies we should be aware of?" I asked before setting the brownies down on a plate.

He shook his head again.

I waited until they were both seated at the table, happily eating brownies and drinking milk before I mentioned the secret ingredient.

Diantha dropped her brownie and stared at me, her eyes wide. "You tricked me with vegetables?"

"I told you I was going to use the beets to make the chocolate fudge."

"But you didn't tell us they were in these brownies." She sounded indignant.

Caleb was smiling at Diantha as she pretended to be offended but then gave in and continued eating her brownie. "I think they're really good, Dahlia," he said.

"Thank you, Caleb. Not everyone has an elevated palate, I guess."

"Hey," Diantha said, laughing.

I went back to cleaning up, and was happy to hear Diantha and Caleb falling into easy conversation about school. As I shut off the water I'd been using to scrub the brownie pan, I heard Diantha say, "but I just don't get why you hide like that, is all."

"Sometimes you see really interesting things. Or hear things," Caleb said.

"Like what?"

"Like the day Mrs. Withers died. The bake sale?"

I kept drying the already dry pan, my back to the kids at the table, but it was impossible not to take a tiny step closer.

"What did you see?"

"I was in this cave—a bunch of us like to go in there and run through this tunnel we found." Caleb had lowered his voice, and I could tell he was trying to see if I was listening. I purposely put the brownie pan down on the counter noisily and began humming to myself. "Anyway, I saw Mrs. Withers go down there to the cove. It was weird, because it was pretty close to when the water comes in. I like watching the tide come, so I go down there sometimes to see it."

"You saw her?" Diantha sounded shocked. "You told the police, right?"

Caleb was silent a moment, and then Diantha said.

"So what else did you see?"

"I saw the janitor yell at her, and she yelled back, and then I saw the principal go down there after her."

Diantha said nothing, but I could imagine the face she might be making. Maybe it was similar to mine, which I was sure was one of surprise.

"And I saw him push her into the water and then she socked him in the face."

"She did?" Diantha sounded impressed.

"Hard, yeah. But then..." Caleb trailed off. "I sort of ran."

"So you didn't see the rest?"

"I didn't want to."

"Scary, huh?" Diantha asked, her voice lowering with sympathy.

"I guess."

"Guys?" I asked, giving up the pretense of cleaning. "When the timer dings, will you take out the pudding?"

"Sure, Aunt Dolly," Diantha said.

"I'll be right back," I told them. And I went to my bedroom to call Owen.

"But it doesn't make sense," Owen said. "We saw Principal Bentley at the festival."

"Owen, I think we actually saw his twin brother," I said. "The principal told me he lives here in town, and that they're very close and people often mistake them for each other. Plus," I went on, "Diantha and I saw one of them at the farmer's market, and he appeared to have a broken nose. I think that's how Dorothy broke her hand."

"So who had the broken nose? Principal Bentley or his brother?"

"I think that's the question at the heart of all of this."

"It seems clear that it's one of them," Owen said. "But we're still missing a motive. Dorothy wouldn't have known about the money missing from the sale, since the tallies hadn't come in when she was killed. She couldn't have threatened him with exposure about the money."

"True, but she had been gathering evidence from previous years," I said, my mind spinning. There were still pieces that didn't make sense. "I don't know the motive, but I don't see any reason for this kid to lie about what he saw."

"Why wouldn't he have come forward earlier?"

"Owen," I said. "He's just a kid."

"Yeah." Owen sounded tired now. "I'll go pick up Principal Bentley."

"And his brother," I said.

"Yep. I'll send a unit to get him so we pick them up at the same time. That way neither of them can warn the other."

"Smart."

"Talk soon."

I hung up, wishing I could figure out the last few details that were bothering me. Who had I talked to at the school about the money? Was it the principal who had been hit in the jaw as Dorothy Withers fought for her life? Or could it have been his brother? But then which one was at the farmer's market with the broken nose and the salt stains on his shoes?

I sank into the chair at the little desk in my bedroom to think, and my hand went automatically to the mouse to wake up my computer. On the screen, an email waited for me from Amanda Steele.

Chapter Twenty-Three

Amanda's email laid out everything she and Daisy had managed to find, and it was more than enough to implicate several powerful people in town, including Principal Bentley. I figured it was good that the police were already on the way to pick him up.

At least seven historical buildings on the peninsula where Saltcliff lay had been bought up in the last ten years by one company, which bore the name, "Mariners Inc."

If nothing else, it explained some of the confusion I'd run into about whether the Mariners were or were not an active organization. The list of properties they'd acquired, most of which had been resold at exorbitant profit, did not include the lighthouse. Despite the fact that it would have felt like that string had been nicely tied up if the building had been among the acquisitions, I was glad not to find it on the list.

I typed a note back to Amanda, suggesting she go ahead with the story on her own if she still had an interest in publishing it. I thought it was what Daisy would have wanted her to do.

Before I headed back into the kitchen to see what the kids were up to, I picked up a couple shoeboxes from Daisy's closet. Was it possible that dioramas still required shoeboxes in the age of the internet? I carried them out to the kitchen just in case.

"Oh, perfect," Diantha said, seeing the boxes. "We were just wondering where to actually build the thing."

Caleb had a laptop open on the kitchen table, and they had a page of notes they'd clearly been making from their research.

"Do you happen to have construction paper and glue?" Caleb asked us.

"Oh, Mom does!" Diantha said, and sprang off her chair. She disappeared and I peered out the kitchen doorway to see her digging in the bottom shelf of a book-case in the living room where there were a couple woven baskets set on top of other boxes. At some point, I'd need to go through all that and tidy it up, but I hadn't felt quite up to it since my sister had died. She returned with scissors, glue, paper, and a few other things. "Craft supplies," she explained, throwing me a smile before setting them all down on the table.

"You guys look like you have everything you need," I said.

"We're good, thanks."

For a moment, I stood in the doorway, the scent of persimmon still hanging in the air and my niece and her friend engaged in deep conversation about kelp beds as they began cutting. Their laughter lifted something heavy inside me and a strange longing shot through my chest. I wished Daisy were here. I wished we could have all experienced this together, this sense of... family. It felt like I'd come home, finally, after such a long time. But my sister wasn't here.

The evening was quiet, and there was no word from Owen about progress on the case. I tried to sleep, but found myself tossing and turning, and rose early to make iced lemon scones to put out with the waffles and scrambled eggs for the guests.

I took Taco out for a walk while the village of Saltcliff was still quiet, a layer of fog settled heavy over the cobbled streets creating a muffled kind of veil that made everything seem mystical and dreamlike. We strolled along Nutmeg, turned down Clove, and finally made our way back up Ginger, coming back to the inn.

Marcus was already at work in the garden, and there were several plants in pots along the path that looked ready for planting. "Almost back to where we started, Dahlia."

I looked around at what had once been a wildly blooming English garden. It didn't look like we were back to me. "It's so sparse," I said sadly, feeling more than ever that Daisy was slipping away from me.

"Well, we're moving into cooler weather," he said. "Much of the garden will go dormant during the winter months, but it'll stay green and lush—that's the blessing of our little microclimate here. But just wait until springtime."

He stood and stretched his back out. "It was almost a gift, what those vandals did here."

"How do you figure that?" I asked, looking around sadly.

"They forced me to move some things around and rethink the plan a bit. It's better now. You'll see. Your sister, I think, would approve." He said this last bit peering at me with a strange expression, as if he could sense how much I was thinking of my sister.

"I hope so," I said, my voice disappearing inside the words.

Marcus reached out and patted my shoulder gently, and the gesture nearly brought me to tears. My emotions had been much closer to the surface than ever before since coming to this tiny town on the ocean. I wasn't sure what to make of it, but did my best to swallow them down and give him a smile that I hoped looked confident.

Inside the inn, guests were up and about, and Amal was chatting with the Sanfords as they sat at the end of the long table in the dining room. I heard her making suggestions for sights to visit and things to do as I moved behind the desk to see how many reservations we had coming in the following week.

It would be Halloween, and much of the village would be participating in the annual Saltcliff Treat or Treat. The name, I thought, was a little repetitive, but Amal had explained that they preferred to discourage tricks, which often felt a lot like vandalism. Having been the recent recipient of such a trick, I thought I supported the idea.

We'd be full for the holiday, and then we were booked out clear through New Year's, with one single group booking up the entire inn for the week around Christmas. That would be interesting, I thought. It also meant that the bathroom renovation would have to wait.

When Amal returned to the desk, I filled her in on the conversation I'd had with Owen the night before.

"So the principal and his brother are both in custody?" Amal asked.

"I think so, yes."

"Which one of them killed Dorothy Withers?"

"It's kind of confusing. I'm not sure. But one of them did."

She nodded, her nose wrinkling up as if she didn't quite have faith in the outcome of this particular investigation.

"There's another thing too, though," I said. "And I need to walk some papers over to Owen if that's okay."

"Take your time," she said. "No one checking in or out today, so it's going to be pretty quiet once the guests all head out for the day."

I went back into the apartment and forwarded Amanda's email to Owen with a note, and then printed out the records she'd sent and tucked them into my bag.

Soon, Taco and I were walking again, this time through a sunnier version of the village. Once the marine layer lifted in the morning, the sun glimmered off the wet streets, making the town feel clean and new.

We arrived at the police station, and the man at the desk picked up the phone as soon as he saw me. "Dahlia Vale is here, sir."

"You can go back," he said, waving me toward Owen's office.

"Thank you," I said, and Taco and I headed back to where Owen sat at his desk, looking at the screen of his computer.

"I printed them out too, in case that helps," I said, startling him.

"Oh! Dahlia, hi. Thanks."

I set the papers in front of Owen and sank into the seat across from him. "Have you figured it all out?"

He nodded, but didn't look especially happy about it. "I think so, but the whole thing is kinda bananas."

"It is?"

Owen sighed and said, "I'll try to explain it to you. It'll be a good test to see if I've got it all right."

"Okay," I said, eager to hear what he had figured out.

"Principal Bentley did not kill Dorothy Withers."

"Oh," I said, a little bit relieved. "Well, that's good."

"But he is a criminal, nonetheless."

"Less good."

"Right."

I waited while Owen appeared to gather his thoughts.

"Principal Bentley had been skimming off the proceeds from the festival and several other school functions for years, sending that money into a fund used by the company your friend identified. The Mariners Inc."

"Oh, that makes sense," I said, happy to see at least one piece of the puzzle click into place.

"As your sister had figured out, I guess, that organization, which includes quite a few pretty important people around town and in the neighboring towns, were quietly using their governmental powers to devalue historic properties in real estate records in order to buy them through Mariners Inc. for much less than they were worth.

"They could have simply resold them, but to make the whole thing legit, they'd spend a bit of money renovating cosmetic items in the buildings, and then resell them at extreme profits."

"So did that make Principal Bentley rich? Sounds like it would have over a decade."

Owen leaned back in his chair and traced an invisible circle on the top of his desk. "It might have," he said. "Except he had a deadbeat brother to support."

"Tate."

"Right, Tate Bentley. The guy didn't finish school, did a few quick stints in prison, and battled some substance abuse issues. Principal Bentley spent most of the money he was making on rehab and bail for his brother, not to mention paying his rent on and off and flat out giving him money."

"Wow. That's a lot."

"That's why this is hard," Owen said, looking pained.

"The principal was doing something wrong, sure, but he was doing it for a good reason. To help his brother."

I could understand that, maybe now more than ever. "But where does Dorothy Withers come into this?"

"That's where it gets a little nuts." Owen stood, tilting his head at me. "You want some coffee?"

"No thank you."

"Well, I need some for this part." He disappeared out the door for a moment and then sat back down with a paper cup in his hand and a shiny muffin in the other. "These don't even come close to yours, by the way, but I'm starving. I've been here most of the night."

I made a note to bring some muffins to the station the next day. No one should have to eat a muffin that looked like it was made out of plastic.

"So," Owen said, leaning forward now and seeming to warm to his story. "Tate was trying—again—to get his act together. And so he had enrolled in a certificate program at the college that would help him get a job at the freight processing center down at the port."

"Well that's good." I liked the idea of someone pulling themselves up by the bootstraps, making a change for the better.

"It would have been, except he ran into a bit of debt with some gambling, and wasn't focusing much on school."

"Oh no."

"Right. So what does Principal Bentley do?"

"I'm guessing he figured out a way to help him."

"He tried, that's for sure. He grabbed some of the cash from the fund and paid off Tate's debt. And then—" Owen rubbed his chin and smiled wryly at me. "You're not going to believe this part."

"Wait," I said. "Can I guess? I actually think I know exactly what happened."

"Dahlia, if you can guess this, I'll buy you the nicest dinner you can imagine—wherever you want."

I narrowed my eyes at Owen. "That's kind of you, but would I be wrong if I said I thought you might have an ulterior motive with that offer?"

"You would be one hundred percent correct. I'm planning to convince you to have dinner with me again either way once this is all over. I just thought I might sweeten the deal a bit by inspiring your competitive nature."

That made me smile. Owen knew me very well. The thought sent a little giddy swirl through my stomach.

"So tell me your hypothesis."

"Okay," I said, letting my mind work through what I suspected had gone on. "If Tate was failing out of his classwork, I think Principal Bentley might have offered to finish the courses for him, take his tests and pretend to be him, that sort of thing."

"I can't believe you got it right," Owen said, grinning with admiration.

"Which means Tate had to go to Saltcliff School and pretend to be Principal Bentley."

Owen nodded.

"But what I'm guessing is that Dorothy Withers figured out something wasn't right and she confronted him about it."

"You're getting warm," Owen said.

I squeezed my eyes shut and thought. If she had caught on that Tate was not Principal Bentley, she would have told someone. So that wasn't it. I realized what it was. "She confronted him about the money that had been missing from the festival for the last nine years. She threatened to expose him."

"Bingo."

"But it wasn't actually the principal she confronted, it was his brother, Tate. And so..." my mind wheeled, and Daisy's face popped into my head as I considered what one twin might do for another when they were threatened. "So Tate decided he would protect his brother, just as Principal Bentley had been doing for him all these years?"

"I think so, yes."

"So when he saw Dorothy go down to the cove, he realized it was his chance to make sure she stayed quiet."

Owen was smiling at me, and the glimmer in his green eyes looked a lot like pride.

"But we saw him at the festival at the same time..." I thought about that. "Wait, no. We saw Principal Bentley."

Owen touched a tip of his finger to his nose, telling me I was right.

"I'm guessing as soon as Principal Bentley realized what his brother had done, they switched back, so the man I had meetings with was actually Principal Bentley. But the man I saw at the farmer's market was Tate." I thought about that. "He had a broken nose and salt lines on his shoes."

"You figured it out, Dahlia."

I shook my head. "No, wait. But the principal was talking funny—like his jaw hurt. Dorothy's broken hand... I figured she hit him in the jaw. Or did she hit Tate in the nose?"

"She broke Tate's nose. And Principal Bentley just visited with his dentist for an abscessed tooth that was probably pretty darned painful."

"Impressive that he's keeping up with his dental hygiene during all this chaos."

"I don't think he had a choice—when it makes you talk funny, it hurts like a dickens. We have the records of his call to the dentist's emergency line."

Well that made sense. "So...it's over? You've got your murderer in custody."

He sighed. "Looks like," he said. "Where would you like to go to dinner?"

"Wait. One more thing. Who vandalized my garden?"

"That's the one thing I don't know. Neither man would admit to it."

I frowned and looked over at Taco, who grunted from his spot on the floor. I didn't like loose ends, and this one felt personal.

"Is your friend going to publish the article about the Mariners Inc.?"

"I don't know," I said. "I told her she should."

Owen dropped my gaze and his tone was grave. "Heads are gonna roll if she does."

"For the best, probably," I said.

"Yep. Messy, but for the best."

I felt better, now that Dorothy Withers's murderer had been identified, but I would have preferred to have all the answers at once—about the garden, about Daisy's strange note... I let out a long sigh.

"Dinner?" Owen said, and there was something so hopeful in his gaze that my heart softened a bit. Whatever I was afraid of, it wasn't him. I genuinely liked Owen—and maybe, if he was as genuine and patient as I though the was—there was a chance for something real to grow between us.

"Yes," I said. "Saturday?"

"You're on. You pick the place?"

I nodded. "Congratulations on solving the case," I said as I stood.

"I'm honestly more excited to have convinced you to go out with me again."

My cheeks heated and I ducked my head so that my hair blocked the furious blush from Owen's view.

"I'll see you Saturday," I told him, risking one last glance into those emerald eyes.

His smile was wide and warm. "See you then."

Chapter Twenty-Four

"So another date?" Amal asked this in a calm voice, as if she had no real interest in the answer, but I could feel her eyes on me as I arranged the afternoon cookies and tea on the sideboard in the lobby. I'd filled her in on everything Owen had told me, and all that I'd figured out about the case.

"That's your question? After I just explained the most insane identity switch of a murder ever?"

Now she smiled, shifting her weight to one hip. "I knew that would get solved. I'm more interested in your relationship with the handsome detective."

I wasn't sure I wanted intense interest in my not-very-exciting and up until now non-existent dating life. "He asked me out for Saturday."

"And you are... happy?"

I sighed. I wanted to be happy. I was happy, I thought.

"Dahlia?"

I stopped the compulsive arranging of tiny tarts on the tray before me and turned, meeting Amal's sympathetic gaze. "I don't know?"

"Sit." Amal waved me to the sofa and we sat, facing one another before the low glow of the fire.

"Tell me what you're feeling when you think about going out with Owen Sanderson."

I dropped her eyes, my own focusing on my fingers twisting together in my lap. "This is embarrassing."

"There's no reason why it should be. Interpersonal relationships of all kinds are what make human life bearable and even enjoyable. We're social creatures, Dahlia. We're not made to be alone."

I knew she was right, and I forced myself to look up, to have this conversation. "I don't really know how I feel." I dug deep, tried to sort through the confusion within me, comforted by Amal's familiar presence and soothing attitude.

"When I see him, I'm happy. And nervous. And kind of...scared?"

"That's totally normal when you like someone. Surely you've felt that before?"

"Yes, but usually from a very safe distance. No one has ever been interested in me that way, I don't think." I glanced over to where my dog lay in a heap on his bed. He was the only close relationship I really had with anyone of the opposite gender. Sad, but true.

"Well, I am an unbiased observer who can tell you that Owen has similar feelings for you."

"Why does that feel so scary?"

"Because it's the unknown, maybe? If you've never been in a romantic relationship, you don't know what to expect."

I nodded. I didn't like situations where I didn't know what to expect. I was awkward enough when I knew exactly what to expect. "That makes sense."

"I think the important thing to know is how you feel. The rest will come naturally and if you're open with Owen about wanting to take things slowly, I know he'll understand."

"I guess..." I ducked my head again. "I just don't know anything about what comes between this part, where my stomach flips and I get hot when he's around, and the people I see on the street who are walking and holding hands and who just look like it's so easy."

"The blanks will fill in naturally," Amal assured me. "Try to live the moments you have with him instead of thinking so hard about everything?"

I scoffed. "Overthinking is my greatest capability."

"That is not true," Amal said, rising to get one of the tiny lemon tarts I'd made. "Baking might be your greatest. Or taking good care of your niece."

"It's in the top five."

"Okay. Well, I'm here if you need me, not that I have a lot more experience than you do."

That actually made me feel better in some strange way. "Thanks."

We spent another hour or two on daily tasks before Diantha came through the front door in a kind of exhausted frenzy. She carried a backpack and the diorama she and Caleb had made, and dropped them both on the desk as she dropped to her knees to greet Taco Dog.

"How was school?" I asked.

She sighed dramatically. "Rhetorical question."

"Not rhetorical. I'm asking."

"It's the same, Aunt Dolly." Her voice wasn't an irritated whine, but it was close, and I kept my eyes on her until she glanced at me again, her face softening. "We got an A on the diorama presentation."

"That's great," I said, willing to let her off the hook with that little bit of information. Before I could tell her to get a snack, the front door of the inn opened again, and Caleb sulked in, followed by a tall man who kept one hand on the boy's shoulder.

"Hello," Amal said.

"Caleb, congratulations, Danny just told me about the diorama presentation," I said.

Caleb glanced up at me and whispered, "thanks."

"I'm Sebastian. Caleb's father," the man said. "Caleb

would like to tell you something." These words were directed at me.

"Oh, erm. Okay." I waited, but Caleb only stared at the floor shifting his weight.

Diantha rose and came over to stand at my side. "What's up, Caleb?"

Caleb sniffed loudly and I noticed his father give his shoulder a firm squeeze as he whispered, "Son."

After another painful pause, Caleb raised a teary gaze to meet mine. "I need to tell you something. About your garden."

"About my garden?" I shook my head, unsure what this could be about.

"I ruined it. Me and some other kids."

Well. I had not expected that. "It was you?" I tried to keep the shock from my voice. "But Caleb, why?"

He sniffed loudly again and then sighed. "We were using the tunnels and the room down under your hotel," he said. "And when you went in there and started figuring things out, we knew you'd tell someone."

I stared at him. "You were in the room beneath the hotel? The speakeasy?"

He squinted at me. "It was like a bar, I think."

He didn't know what a speakeasy was. "Right. An old bar."

"We hung out in there sometimes. Played D&D and stuff."

So it had been the kids in the tunnels who had been in the speakeasy. Those were the footprints I'd seen.

"But why destroy the garden?"

Caleb dropped his gaze again. "It wasn't my idea, but one of the guys said if you thought it was bad guys threatening you, maybe you wouldn't tell anyone about the tunnels."

"It worked," I told him.

He raised his chin. "It didn't work. The tunnels are all shut down!"

"Well, I mean you did scare me. And I did think it was something a little more serious."

He nodded.

"But those tunnels are really old and probably not safe," I told him.

"We've discussed that," Sebastian said. "Caleb would like to compensate you for the damage."

I didn't have the heart to tell him how much I'd paid Marcus to buy new plants for the garden. "That's not necessary," I said.

"It is," Sebastian assured me. "But if you're not comfortable with money, perhaps Caleb could work in the garden? Help get it put back together?"

I wondered how Marcus would feel about having help. "I think that might be arranged. I'll speak with the gardener and let you know," I told them.

"For what it's worth, I'm sorry too," Sebastian said.

"You think you're doing a good job parenting, but then you just don't always know what kids are up to."

I glanced at Diantha, and then back at Sebastian. "It's okay," I said. "I appreciate the information and the apology."

"Sorry, Danny," Caleb whispered, not meeting Diantha's eye.

"It's okay," she said, sounding more than ready to forgive her friend.

"We'll let you get on with your day then," Sebastian said, turning back to the door of the inn.

When they'd left, Amal smiled at me. "One more mystery solved."

That night Diantha lay sprawled across my bed, the snow globe in her hands and the note in front of her.

"It really doesn't mean anything to you? Maybe it's something from when you were kids?" She asked me.

I propped myself up on one elbow, staring at the numbers. "We did have some kind of code, but I don't remember exactly how it worked."

Diantha's eyes widened. "Hang on. I want to hear this song." She went to the bathroom and returned with a pair of tweezers, which she used to wind the mechanism on the bottom of the globe. A moment later, the tinny notes of Twinkle, Twinkle Little Star flittered in the air.

"That was it," I said, the memory coming back to me slowly. "It was that song."

"Twinkle, Twinkle Little Star?" Diantha asked doubtfully.

I nodded, pulling a notepad from the nightstand. "What was it? Something about the syllables."

I wrote out the words to the song, breaking up the syllables. "If I remember correctly, each syllable has a number, so the first syllable is one, the next is two, etcetera."

"Easy enough," Diantha said.

"And each number represents the letter the syllable starts with."

"So you don't get that many letters," Diantha pointed out. "There's not a lot you can spell."

"True," I agreed. I remembered stretching a bit in the way we applied the code. "You can use other songs. But this was the first one we made up." A wash of warmth came over me as I remembered curling up with Daisy in a tent we'd pitched behind Grandmother's porch on a summer evening. We had a flashlight and a notebook, and that was where we came up with our code. How could I have forgotten it?

"So, can you crack Mom's code then?" Diantha asked, picking up the slip of paper.

"Maybe. Read me the numbers."

"The first on is three," she said.

"So that would be T. For Twin, the third syllable in the song."

"Okay. Write that down. Next is 13."

"That would be A," I said.

We continued, deciphering each number according to the syllables, and ended with a word that was not a word.

"TALASYAL?" Diantha read it out loud. "That makes no sense." Then she looked up at me, and her eyes grew sad. "Mom was pretty sick at the end..."

I shook my head. "No, this is what I meant. Sometimes you have to stretch the rules a little bit. We just have to figure out what else those letters could be based on the other letters in the syllables the numbers represent."

"Oh. So like 13 is 'are,' so that could actually be A or R or E?"

"Right. And we used 5 for E because it is the last letter of syllable five and syllable three is already T."

"Okay," Diantha said slowly. "Your code wasn't exactly foolproof, Aunt Dolly."

"We were kids," I said, excitedly working through the possibilities until I thought maybe I had it. "Do you think the word could be TREASURE?"

Diantha went through the syllables, checking to see if

there was a likely swap for each one that made my guess work. "It could be," she said. "But what does that mean?"

I rolled onto my back, thinking. "Well, when we were kids, we had a little treasure box and if the word was 'booty' or 'prize,' or anything like that, the thing we hid would always be in there."

Diantha popped up to a sitting position suddenly, startling Taco. "We have a treasure box!"

"You do?"

"Yeah, come with me." She leapt off the bed and I followed her through the apartment to the bookcase where she'd dug out the art supplies a few days earlier. "It's in here."

Diantha shuffled several baskets and books to the ground, and pulled out the little treasure box I remembered from my childhood.

"I can't believe Daisy still has this," I laughed.

"What's in it?"

I was almost afraid to open it. Was this really what Daisy wanted me to find? I smiled at my niece, took a deep breath, and lifted the lid. Inside was an envelope with my sister's loopy script spelling out "Dahlia."

For no discernible reason, tears sprang to my eyes.

"A letter?"

I nodded.

"Anything for me?" Diantha asked.

I pulled the letter out and peered into the little box,

which was empty. I looked at my niece, afraid she'd be disappointed, and shook my head.

"That's okay. Mom left me lots of things," she said, smiling at me. "This is for you."

I closed the treasure chest and put it back on the shelf, holding the letter carefully.

"I'm going to take Taco out to the garden," Diantha said. "We'll be back in a minute." She slipped out the door with the dog, leaving me alone with my sister's letter.

I sank into a soft armchair and slid my finger beneath the flap, pulling out a sheet of paper covered in my sister's handwriting.

Dear Dahlia:

There's no real excuse for this letter coming several years later than it should have, so I'll start with something I should have said years ago. I'm sorry.

I know it has been more than a decade since I've really talked to you, and I've come to realize what a horrific mistake I made in keeping you at a distance.

Despite the pain I think it may have caused, please know that I did what I thought was best at the time.

I got my diagnosis a decade ago. And I didn't tell anyone. No one. I barely acknowledged it myself. Amal and I hadn't met yet, and the only person I really had besides you was Danny, who was only a baby. So I kept my illness a secret, and finally opted to treat it quietly, secretly. I didn't want sympathy, but more than that—I didn't want to be sick. So I tried to tell myself I wasn't.

Those first rounds of chemo and radiation were awful, but they did the trick. The thing was, they made me so sick, I could barely function. If I'd called you then, or let you see me, you'd have known. So I kept quiet, but I didn't have energy for anything besides going to treatment and caring for Danny.

The thing about cancer—I guess especially if you don't deal with it—is that it also affects your mental health. And I was a mess. I felt guilt, shame, disappointment, and all of this while I was doing my best to raise a happy and healthy little girl by myself.

Dahlia, I love you. You are half my heart and always have been—but you struggle to understand anything that isn't straightforward, black and white. And whatever was going on in my mind was far from that. I couldn't explain it to myself, so how could I explain it to you?

Time passed, and I got sick again when Danny was eight. She remembers a little bit of it, but I did my best to hide it again, denying to anyone that there was anything wrong. But my soul ached.

That's when I met Amal, when I was just coming back out of treatment that second time. She was so strong and confident and sure, and so very reassuring. She took my messy fears and straightened them out, and she made me a better person.

But she couldn't convince me that dragging you back into my life would do anything except confuse and worry you.

I know now that I should have listened to her. That I stole a decade from us both. When the cancer came again, I knew I wouldn't be able to fight it. And I knew it was too late to reach out to you. Too much had already happened, and each time, I worried I'd drag you into it all only to die and have you feel like you should have done something more, something that would be impossible for anyone. You always took on more responsibility than you should.

So now, I guess I'm counting on that trait. I'm counting on your ability to forgive me, and your willingness to take on my responsibilities. I didn't want to leave them. I didn't want to leave you. But Dahlia, will you please do what I couldn't do?

Raise my daughter?

Care for her like your own?

And please, please... tell me you forgive me.

Love,

· · ·

Your sister, Daisy

I wiped tears from my cheeks and stared at the letter.

Ten years.

For no real reason at all.

I thought it was possible I actually felt my heart break inside my chest.

Chapter Twenty-Five

On Saturday night, I convinced Owen that I didn't need a fancy dinner at all. Instead, we drove to Monterey, walked through the aquarium, and had an early dinner in a seafood restaurant near the pier. It was casual and fun, and the aquarium provided plenty of distraction from whatever lay between us.

Owen held my hand as we strolled, and I let myself enjoy it, let the warmth of his nearness fill me with something like security.

Over dinner, I confessed my fears about the relationship. Probably not in a very articulate manner—that was kind of how I operated.

Owen listened, the bright green eyes holding mine and the smile never fading from his face. When I'd managed to get out the words, he nodded.

"Dahlia," he said, "I have never met anyone quite like

you. The last thing I'd ever want is to make you feel uncomfortable or rushed. I believe you and I are a good fit, just as we are."

"You're not... waiting for more?" I asked, my mind racing through the continuum of relationship landmarks popularized by modern culture—movies, media, songs.

Owen shrugged and sat back in his chair, running a hand through his hair and making the waves fall softly around his forehead. "I guess I'm looking for something a little deeper," he said. "I never want you to doubt how attractive you are to me, though. But I respect you far too much, and care much too much about our friendship and our intellectual relationship to overstep in any other way."

I stared at him, wondering if what he said could possibly be true. Both the parts about finding me attractive, and about caring more about the other aspects of our relationship. "Really?"

He laughed. "Yes, really."

I couldn't help but stare at him. How had I gotten so lucky?

That evening, Owen drove Taco and me back to the inn, and walked us to the door. When Taco dropped into a sit as I said goodnight, Owen leaned over to pat his head, and I leaned forward, meeting his lips with my own.

Owen froze, and then his hand landed lightly on my hip before he stood back up.

My entire body felt warm and buzzy, even though I

hadn't had a drink. "Thank you," I said, and I wondered if he knew that I meant for absolutely everything. For involving me in the puzzles he solved for work, for including me as an equal in conversations, for his patience and his warmth, for the kind things he said.

"Thank you, Dahlia," he said, grinning at me.

"Will you join us tomorrow?" I asked. The next day was the annual Treat or Treat, and we were expecting quite a few visitors at the inn.

"You bet," he said. "I can't wait to see Taco's costume."

I laughed. Poor Taco. Diantha had gotten her way in the end.

"This is amazing!" Diantha stood next to me at the front arch of the inn's garden at six o'clock, the appointed hour for the village's annual Treat or Treat to kick off. Owen was on my other side, and Amal was seated at a table just behind where we'd stepped out to get a view of the street.

People ambled everywhere, dressed in costumes. The lights strung over Nutmeg were lit and every shop window glimmered and glowed. Children carried hollow pumpkins and pillowcases, and stopped by each store for goodies, while their parents partook of the goods being sold by street vendors with candy apples, popcorn, and cider.

We had hot chocolate and cake pops laid out for visitors, and Taco laid morosely beneath the table, clearly embarrassed about his costume.

"Doll!" Sylvan ambled up the sidewalk, Luigi at his side.

I couldn't suppress the laugh that bubbled out of me as I took in his costume. Sylvan wore an enormous fruited turban and diaphanous harem pants in a silky texture with gold shoes that turned up the toes. His top half was wrapped in a gold material, and he held a gold genie lamp in one hand. Luigi had on a similar costume, his wrinkled legs sporting a boot version of the genie shoes and a tiny turban strapped to his head.

"You look amazing," Amal said, coming to greet him.

"Thanks," Sylvan said, preening. "And let's see here... Danny girl, excellent pirate. I see you got the peg leg and everything. Detective," he said to Owen, who was dressed as a circus ringmaster with a tall top hat, bright purple jacket and a cane. Amal and I both wore witch costumes she and Daisy had gotten a few years back. Taco wandered out to greet his friend, and Sylvan burst into laughter.

"Oh my, Taco, what a fitting costume."

Taco lifted his head to look up at Sylvan with a resigned amber gaze, his guacamole hat slipping to one side.

My dog was dressed as a taco, in a costume Diantha had found online and insisted he would adore. Taco had spent most of the evening trying to remove the enormous shell from around his body and finally hiding from sight.

Sylvan and Diantha continued chatting, and Owen stepped out to speak to some other revelers stopping by. Amal smiled at me and linked her arm through mine as we stood in the new growth of Daisy's garden.

"I talked to the contractor," she said, as if she'd just remembered to tell me. "He thinks they can get the speakeasy ready to go and the back entrance in place before the holidays."

"So soon?" I asked, surprised. We'd agreed to put off bathroom renovations, since we were full through New Years, but we'd decided that getting the bar operational would be another revenue stream and a fun attraction for guests and visitors. We'd agreed to create a new entrance in the back of the property on the alley so visitors didn't have to come through the inn itself.

"Yep," Amal said, smiling. "They'll be starting next week."

"Great."

Soon, the garden was full of visitors chatting and laughing, and the streets of my adopted hometown glowed with light and love. The smells of the nearby ocean mingled with wafting cinnamon and that singularly fall scent of fallen leaves and approaching cooler weather.

As I gazed around me, I realized how rich my life had become since coming to Saltcliff by the Sea, and my heart swelled with happiness. With the painful exception of my twin sister, I had everything I'd ever wanted, right here in this cozy, wonderful place.

Thanks for reading the second Saltcliff Mystery!

Want to see what Dahlia, Danny, and Taco are up to next? Don't miss A Holiday Homicide, the next Saltcliff Mystery! Get it here! And keep reading for recipes straight from the Saltcliff Inn!

Persimmon Pudding Recipe (with High Altitude Adjustment)

Ingredients:

- 2 cups Hachiya persimmon pulp (from about 3-4 ripe persimmons)
- 1 ½ cups sugar
- 2 large eggs
- ½ cup unsalted butter, melted
- 1 ½ cups all-purpose flour
- 1 teaspoon baking soda (reduce to ¾ teaspoon for high altitude)
- ½ teaspoon salt (reduce to ¼ teaspoon for high altitude)
- 1 teaspoon ground cinnamon
- ½ teaspoon ground nutmeg
- ½ teaspoon ground cloves

- 1 cup milk (increase to 1 ¼ cups for high altitude)
- 1 teaspoon vanilla extract
- ½ cup chopped walnuts or pecans (optional)
- Whipped cream or vanilla ice cream, for serving

Instructions:

1. **Preheat the Oven**: Preheat your oven to 325°F (163°C). Grease an 8x8-inch baking dish or a similar-sized pudding mold.

2. **Prepare the Persimmon Pulp**: Scoop the flesh out of the ripe Hachiya persimmons and purée it in a blender or food processor until smooth.

3. **Mix Wet Ingredients**: In a large mixing bowl, combine the persimmon pulp, sugar, and eggs. Stir in the melted butter and mix well.

4. **Combine Dry Ingredients**: In a separate bowl, sift together the flour, baking soda (reduced for high altitude), salt (reduced for high altitude), cinnamon, nutmeg, and cloves.

5. **Combine Everything**: Gradually add the dry ingredients to the wet mixture, alternating with the milk (increased for high altitude), and

stir until smooth. Add the vanilla extract and, if using, fold in the chopped nuts.

6. **Bake**: Pour the batter into the prepared baking dish and smooth the top. Bake in the preheated oven for 60-70 minutes (check at 55 minutes at high altitude), or until a toothpick inserted into the center comes out clean.

7. **Cool and Serve**: Let the pudding cool slightly before serving. Serve warm with a dollop of whipped cream or a scoop of vanilla ice cream.

Chocolate Beet Cake Recipe (with High Altitude Adjustment)

I ngredients:

- 1 cup cooked and puréed beets (about 2 medium beets)
- 1 cup sugar
- ½ cup vegetable oil
- 2 large eggs
- 1 teaspoon vanilla extract
- 1 ½ cups all-purpose flour
- ½ cup unsweetened cocoa powder
- 1 ½ teaspoons baking soda (reduce to 1 ¼ teaspoons for high altitude)
- ¼ teaspoon salt (reduce to ⅛ teaspoon for high altitude)
- ½ cup buttermilk (increase to ⅔ cup for high altitude)

- ½ cup semi-sweet chocolate chips (optional)

Instructions:

Preheat the Oven: Preheat your oven to 350°F (175°C). Grease and flour an 8-inch round cake pan.

Prepare the Beets: If you haven't already, cook the beets until tender (boiling or roasting works well), then purée them in a food processor or blender until smooth.

Mix Wet Ingredients: In a large mixing bowl, combine the beet purée, sugar, oil, eggs, and vanilla extract. Mix until well combined.

Combine Dry Ingredients: In a separate bowl, sift together the flour, cocoa powder, baking soda (reduced for high altitude), and salt (reduced for high altitude).

Combine Everything: Gradually add the dry ingredients to the wet mixture, alternating with the buttermilk (increased for high altitude), and stir until just combined. If using, fold in the chocolate chips.

Bake: Pour the batter into the prepared cake pan and smooth the top. Bake in the preheated oven for 30-35 minutes (check at 28 minutes at high altitude), or until a toothpick inserted into the center comes out clean.

Cool and Serve: Let the cake cool in the pan for about 10 minutes, then turn it out onto a wire rack to cool completely. Dust with powdered sugar or frost with your favorite chocolate frosting, if desired.

More Nancy

The Saltcliff Mystery Series:

Book 1: Keeled Over at the Cliffside

What happens when Gilmore Girls meets Murder, She Wrote?
You get Dahlia Vale and snarky Diantha along with Taco Dog
solving murders in the Saltcliff Mystery series! Follow along as
Dahlia builds her community and family, and solves mysteries
along the way. You'll love the small town vibe, B&B setting, and
romantic sub-plot in this cozy culinary series!

The Windthorne Witches Series:

Book 1: All Hallows Hex

Wine, Witches, and all kinds of Weird... What's a midlife witch
to do when her peaceful magical life is upended by murder?

In the cozy wine town of Moonridge, California, magic flows as
freely as the local vintages—and for the Windthorne sisters, it's
the key to their family's success. Filled with sisterhood, humor,
and heart, this series is the perfect mix of cozy mystery and
paranormal intrigue. If you love witchy vibes, midlife magic,
and small-town charm, join the Windthorne witches as they face
down ancient secrets, dark forces, and the challenges of everyday
life—one spell at a time.

Other Books - Steamy Small Town Romance written as Delancey Stewart

The Wilcox Wombats Series:

Book 1: The Wedding Winger

Ready for some ha ha with your hockey? The Wilcox Wombats bring the camaraderie and sense of found family you're looking for, along with snort-laughs and swoons. The first book features a star winger planning for his future, but caught up in the past. When his high school touch (the smart girl who always thought he was just a dumb jock) moves back next door, he knows he's in trouble. Grab it here!

The Kasper Ridge Series:

Free Prequel: Only a Summer

Book 1: Only a Fling

Read the Kasper Ridge Series to get your fill of small town steam with plenty of humor! Former fighter pilots share deep bonds and plenty of inside jokes. Step into their world as they join together to help renovate the Kasper Ridge Resort, a dilapidated mountain property in Colorado, left as an inheritance to Ghost, one of their own. But the inheritance also comes with a treasure hunt! Each book follows a different couple but each story builds another link in the hunt, so read them in order! Start with Only a Summer, which is free! Then pick up Only a Fling here.

The Singletree Series:

Book 1: Happily Ever His

What happens when the totally normal sister of a movie starlet meets her ultimate movie star crush, only to find out he is dating her famous sister? But it gets a bit more complicated than that.

Tess's sister has brought movie hottie Ryan home for her grandmother's 90th birthday to show the world how quickly she could move on after her very public divorce. The relationship is just for show... but Tess doesn't know that at first. And Gran? Is a video gaming, weed smoking, take-no-prisoners firecracker who tells it like it is. Toss in a lovesick chicken, and you're on your way to understanding what kind of series Singletree promises to be.

Plan to laugh. Pick up book 1 here!

The MR. MATCH Series:

Free Prequel: Scoring a Soulmate

Book 1: Scoring the Keeper's Sister

If you enjoy a side of sports with your sexy men, and want both wrapped up in a hilarious package, then you're going to love Mr. Match. Soccer star and genius Max Winchell has discovered the formula for love and built a dating app around it. Though he keeps his identity secret, he convinces all his teammates to try it... and one after another, they fall in love. First up? Fernando "the fire" Fuerte, who shares an enemies-to-lovers romance with PR rep Erica, who happens to be his teammates twin sister. Taboo, forced proximity, and tons of witty banter up the steam in this one! Get it here!

The KINGS GROVE Series:

Book 1: When We Let Go

Coming right up, a bit of Sequoia mountain steam mixed with small town swoon! Head to Kings Grove for quirky side characters, emotional love stories, happy ever afters, and a cast you'll want to make your neighbors. Book 1 features Maddie returning to her childhood home, only to be swept off her feet by a handsome and potentially dangerous stranger. These books are steamy and engaging, with a touch of humor. Read book 1 here!

THE GIRLFRIENDS OF GOTHAM Series:

Book 1: Men and Martinis

Head to to the dot-com heyday of NYC - the late 1990s! Join Natalie Pepper as she makes her way in the big city in this Carrie Bradshaw meets Bridesmaids coming of age story. Meet the girlfriends here!

The Digital Dating Series (with Marika Ray):

Book 1: Texting with the Enemy

Looking for sweet romance with a romcom kick? That's what you get when Delancey and Marika Ray team up! In this series starter, Elle is texting a guy she isn't sure she likes, but boy does he give good text. The only problem? She's actually texting her boss since "the guy" gave her his buddy's number instead of his own. Now she's falling slowly in love with the perfect guy and can't figure out why he doesn't seem perfect in person... Needless to say, hilarity ensues. Pick it up here!

Made in the USA
Monee, IL
06 March 2025

13588182R00157